THE
Great American Rabbit Chase

THE
Great American
Rabbit Chase

Pat Parsons

CONTENTS

Dedication..vii
Preface..ix

Chapter 1 – Discovering the Rabbit.. 1
Chapter 2 – A Taste of Rabbit... 4
Chapter 3 – Receiving My Education 8
Chapter 4 – Nymphomania Lover 26
Chapter 5 – Talanted Tongue Travel..32
Chapter 6 – Tickle–Tickle Pee Pee...38
Chapter 7 – The Getaway 48
Chapter 8 – The Sexy Sister 52
Chapter 9 – My Slot Machine Lover...60
Chapter 10 – My Cherie...73
Chapter 11 – Sister Love..81
Chapter 12 – "A Motorized Menage a trois" 93
Chapter 13 – My Ultimate Lovemaking Training Program 102

DEDICATION

"The Great American Rabbit Chase"

This was a title I chose that would equate or relate to a very large part of my life. This book is dedicated to all the people who were kind enough to assist me in my lustful quest for making love. That would include those who somehow became in charge of the different training programs I put myself through. It would also include all participants, no matter how overzealous some may have been. The overzealous ones were very special, and so much more enlightening and fun to learn from. When one becomes overzealous in the art of making love, there are no limits. Very simply put, it is very easy to **MAX OUT!!!**

It would also include my friends that help me put this book together. They were persons of strong constitutional beliefs, yet they were in control enough to keep an open mind and not try to influence me to make changes in any way.

It is extremely difficult to single out one individual for this dedication. Since I feel I must, I give total dedication and responsibility, love and appreciation, to that wonderful

"Boss Lady"!!!

She was truly a lust-filled love-crazy sexy bitch. I do not know who "They" are, but they say, (it takes one to know one)-and-(birds of a feather flock together). Thank you, my darling

Becky, it was my great pleasure knowing you and even a greater treasure to have you as a best friend!!!

I also thank you for those wonderfully special and precious times you flocked with me. I never have nor shall I ever forget you!!!

Forever, Pat

"✳✳✳✳✳✳✳✳✳✳✳✳✳✳✳✳✳✳✳✳✳✳✳✳✳✳"

PREFACE

"The Great American Rabbit Chase"

This book reveals the first part of a story about how a little boys interest in a certain body part belonging to the opposite sex became the dominant force of his life. This part was once referred to as a rabbit, hence the name of the book. The body part had such magnetic powers over him that it controlled his mind for the better part of his childhood, youth, and young adulthood. Learning more and more about this particular body part began to open doors and he became enlightened and educated about certain other body parts. Living to the pleasures of these parts presented him with unwanted punishment at times. He became quite interested in how to perform and exist continuously punishment free. For one reason or another, his chosen path of travel in life could never completely be punishment free. He came to realize his continued pursuit for acquiring the skills to achieve a goal he has set for himself would always present the possibility of mental, physical, or heartfelt pain at one point or another. Since she had no control over the situation, he knew he would just have to accept that was the way it was going to be. As he got better and better at his craft, what once upon a time was an interest became an addiction. One that was projected with almost every sound and move he made. When his marriage failed, he decided to make it a lifelong dream to try to please every woman that he possibly could.

Having achieved a large part of that lifelong dream, he felt the obligation to convey many stories of the happiness and pleasure's he received along the way.

"AND SO HERE WE ARE!!!"

CHAPTER 1

Discovering the Rabbit

I t all began when I was about three years old. My mother had
taken ill and was in the hospital. During that time, I was staying
with my grandmother and grandfather at the family manor
house. My aunt and uncle and their children were living there also.
I guess it was to make sure grandma and grandpa had enough
help on the farm. They were getting older and my grandfather had
been in some kind of an accident. I'm not sure what happened, but
sometimes his mouth wouldn't say what he was thinking.

It was late in the evening after supper. Back then the evening
meal was referred to as supper not dinner. As usual, the family
had gathered around in the living room by the warmth of a rather
large potbellied stove. I was lying on the floor with the dog looking
up in the air and around at all the people sitting in kind of like a
little circle. A couple neighbor families had just arrived. They were
all singing and having the families evening devotions. Suddenly
something caught my eye. I guess I wasn't quite sure what it was, so
I kept watching it. It wasn't very long until I felt myself being lifted
up off the floor and pressed against my aunt's breast. I remember

thinking how much larger the place where my head was, compared to what I was used to with my mother. She said, in a laughing kind of way, "What were you looking at Skippy, a rabbit?" By that time the view had changed. I was being held in a position that was like my mother held me when she thought I was hungry. I guess I was trying to find a nipple, because I remember feeling around and finding the little valley that separates one head rest from the other.

Living with my relatives at the Manor house, as I look back on it now, was one of the most enlightening and influential times of my life. I guess because I was so young and my mother was not with me, it became necessary for someone to sleep with me or keep me company during the night. That would be my aunt and uncle. Over the next few months, they taught me about everything I needed to know for me to embark upon my journey through life in pursuit of happiness for myself as well as others.

I remember seeing their shadows in the soft moonlight shining through the window. My uncle was resting his head much the same as I if my mother was preparing me for bed. The only difference was he didn't seem to be sleepy. His hands started moving all over my aunts body. His head was moving around while he was making these vibrating, bubble-bursting, semi-sucking sounds with his lips and tongue on her tummy skin. Then he quickly moved his face to her face and began biting her all around the mouth. Which later became known to me as kissing. Then without warning he started sliding down biting her body everywhere, under her arm, on her arm, on her belly, and slipping on down to her legs. My uncle had both hands under her butt and seemed to be pulling my aunt up to his face while the lower part of his body was moving around and rubbing rather violently on the sheets.

Then all of a sudden, his face almost disappeared. He started making this noise like he was slurping up what was left of a really good bowl of soup. My aunt started moving her head around wildly and grabbing the top and sides of my uncles head with both hands.

She pulled his face in toward her body as she pushed her body toward his face.

The slurping sounds got louder and more intense, and her groaning did the same. Their bodies were flailing around from side to side and up and down. Suddenly my aunt let out a scream and my uncle grunted as the sounds got much louder for a few seconds and then slowly quieted down. It looked like both their bodies were stiff and stretching with the shakes.

By this time, I was sitting up in bed watching them through this kind of cheesecloth netting type material they had stretched halfway over the bed and what appeared to be only around them. As I think about it now, it must have been something commonly used to keep flies and mosquitoes away at night. Then I heard my aunt say, "Oh my "God" honey, look." They both looked over at me. They must've thought I would be asleep. My aunt looked over at me and said, "Lay down Skippy, go back to sleep."

A few days later in the afternoon my aunt and I laid down to take a nap. After a little while I thought she was asleep. I pushed up against the side of her leg and started rubbing it like I saw my uncle do just a few nights before. She of course moved a little and told me to go to sleep I needed to take my nap. I believe she knew what I was doing. After all, they say that children learn by watching.

My aunt and uncle's bedtime manners seemed to be a nightly ritual as they repeatedly performed to each other's pleasure. Many nights it would occur more than once or twice. I became the recipient of many lessons in what was later to become known to me as making love, while watching my aunt and uncle demonstrate for me their own idea of "early to bed and easy to rise."

My aunt and uncle were very loving and wonderful people. They loved each other very much all their life. I didn't know what was going on at the time. But I can tell you now, I am extremely grateful to have been able to take lessons and begin learning the art of making love from two people who were truly in love and cared so very much about pleasing each other.

CHAPTER 2

A Taste of Rabbit

I am putting this all together with the help of my memories and memoirs. It appears there never seemed to be a shortage of young ladies, or for that matter, older ladies who were always willing to accommodate my desires.

When I was younger, four, five, and six, they were next-door neighbors. Or girls my age that may have been attending some church function. Some added attractions that I introduced these young ladies to, really had nothing to do with church. Most likely it had everything to do with anything but church. I would teach them to play some of the same games I had been taught by other young ladies. Games like, doctor and nurse, you show me yours I'll show you mine. Follow the salt-shaker, was my favorite game. We were always running out of salt. I must have been a prime candidate for high blood pressure at age 7. We played games that would benefit the mind by uncovering the body. Plus a few that I had invented as I worked my way through the learning stages of bare-body truth and dare.

I never liked playing with little boys my age. It just wasn't as much fun. I think I already knew at that young age that I was born for fun. Besides, I knew what the boy's body had and looked like. I had absolutely no desire to attempt the healing process by shaking salt on the unknown parts of their body and washing it off with my tongue.

Ages seven, eight, and nine as I recall, began a more risky phase of my exploratory activities. My seventh year was a little rough and very disappointing for me. I suppose the reason I got away with some of the things I did was because I was so young. I believe some people probably thought it was cute, or funny. I soon found out at age 7 it was no longer considered cute, or funny. I got beat up by older brothers and told on by their mothers. I received more face-slapping's and ass beatings the first six months of that year, than the rest of my entire life.

The worst part of it all was my lack of accomplishments. I got very little touching, and only a couple kisses. I did manage one very fruitful performance of touchy-feely, you show me yours I'll show you mine. We got so far out of place and carried away we had to get 2 back-up salt-shaker's and still run out. That relationship was very important to me. I stayed in close touch with that young lady for the next couple years. As a matter of fact, she became my first love. Which I think pissed her older sister off because she had been my teacher a couple years earlier for my cunt-licking class.

My babysitters, however, were a whole different story. They were usually from 3 to 5 years older than I was, and just as curious and playful as I wanted them to be. Being alone with me gave them a free hand without fear of getting caught. By the time I turned nine years old I had been introduced to the Red Snapper. I got my finger bit and my tongue addicted. She was 13 years old and remained my babysitter for the next two years. I suppose if the truth were known, she was my first sex instructor. I still love her and appreciate everything she did for me. I see her every now and then in the grocery store. We smile at each other, say hello, and have a friendly conversation. I can tell by the look in her eyes, as I know she can tell by looking at mine, we are both having what life is all about. A memory from moments of afterglow. (**"Thank you so very much Jean, and welcome to my wonderful world of** *"Afterglow"*!!!**)**

From there I graduated to nurses and candy stripers. I was in one of the major university hospitals having an operation on my arm when all my lucky stars got all lined up in the right order. One of my very attentive and special late-night nurses looked in my eyes and was able to tell that a little hand gesturing massage would probably help keep me from becoming homesick, and so it was.

After a few weeks of persuasively soothing, make you feel at home stimulation recovery, I was transferred to their rehabilitation center. That became my home for the next year and a half. It was a "hole" lot of fun. Anybody that wanted to be happy could be happy there. And that was their intension. The healing process and physical progress go hand-in-hand with happiness.

I had candy stripers available to fill all my needs. And even some that weren't supposed to be included. I could walk just fine but I got private little wheelchair rides, and gentle hand massages while stretching my muscles in the whirlpool machine. Anything I wanted at any time from the kitchen. I had a special bedtime story-teller that also tucked me in every night. She also provided certain pleasurable acts of sex. I enjoyed them so much and she provided them so often that we finally got caught. That of course resulted in her dismissal. She was my favorite little candy striper. I was 13 she was 18, her name was JoAnn and she lived in New York City. She wrote me several letters and we stayed in touch for about a year. I had grown quite fond of her. JoAnn always did everything she could to make me happy. Consequently, I have never been homesick in my life.

There always seemed to be a JoAnn everywhere at the right time in my life. Assisting and allowing me to acquire the knowledge necessary so that I might achieve a point of excellence in performing the many different stages of being respectful to the needs and feelings of my partners. This to me, became the most important part in performing the process of fulfilling the obligation to the art of making love. For example, the responsibility of providing sensual, sexual, stimulation while in the process of performing top-notch excitement for the enticement of an ecstasy filled orgasmic response to the aforementioned art. My objective was to leave them with memories of a pleasurable encounter they would not soon, or maybe never forget.

Some people say all things happen for a reason. Others contend, if you are born under the right sign and your stars are all in line, you will have no problem following the direction in which they lead you. Thereby you will have been given a natural ability to identify with others of the same birthright. I am not sure what the truth really is. I suppose I must lend credence to both theories.

I am also aware of another birthright, that of my father. My father and all seven of his brothers were very horny men. They could not, nor did they attempt to pretend they could be happy with one woman. That is not to mention my mother's side of the family. They seem to have their share of horny people also. My father, through two marriages holds the legal status for being the father of nine children. And we have it on pretty good authority that he holds the honorary father title for five more. He would never admit it totally. My father would just smile and say, "Well you know people tell all kind of stories, some are true and some are not." Some of the ones that were true I went to school with. I got a little too friendly with one particular half sister and her mother let me know it. She told me I was just like my father even the cows were not safe when he was around. I know this because in his later years my father and I became drinking buddies. When a father and son are drinking buddies, they sometimes share much more than their alcohol. I thank my father very much for whatever or how much hormonal input he was able to part with on my behalf.

CHAPTER 3

Receiving My Education

B y the beginning of my sophomore year in high school my recovery was complete. My arm was still a little weak but that was to be expected.

I found that my points of conversation held so much more in common with the young ladies in my class than the boys. I had no desire to excel in sporting events. I did however have a desire to please every girl I possibly could. That desire included not only the young ladies in my class but in the entire high school.

I began writing poetry and started a band. I was in almost every show and talent contest the school held. By my senior year I was voted the most popular boy in school. Who knows, perhaps that was my reward for all those private little poetry recitals I held for my female classmates as we would make our way through the wooded pathways to the park. There I would put on display my talents in other romantic areas. That much like poetry, were also an art. One that I had chosen to someday be worthy of holding the title of Master in the art of making love. Although I knew that title for me was far out of reach at the time. Still, I reached anyway and had become quite polished in my verbal and physical performances to this stage in my life. I was very determined in my pursuit for excellence as my mind traveled in advance to Master status.

Upon graduation from high school I found myself for the first time in somewhat of a stagnant, or semi-limbo status. Perhaps created by the lack of or longing for availability to the opposite sex. The previous four years had spoiled me with what one might call a captive audience due to the mandatory enrollment age policy provided by high school.

In fear of falling into a sexual depression I made it a point to pursue happiness, along with, creating the possibility of furthering my education in the art of making love. It had come to my attention while wondering around aimlessly mulling over my misery filled mind from lack of my favorite activity. There just happened to be quite a large number of very friendly older females in my area that might be willing to make themselves available to participate in a training program with me.

Knowing my knowledge of the avenue I was pursuing, to say the least was incomplete, I chose to set my sights somewhat higher. I was convinced I could acquire a more stimulating education by attending to the wants and needs of the ladies who might just be willing to bestow upon me their knowledge of sexual satisfaction.

I had just got a job at one of the most popular major grocery stores around. It seemed to be very clear to me that husbands or male friends usually did not accompany their spouses or counterparts while they were grocery shopping.

It was a perfect situation. I could sharpen my flirtatious mannerisms while assisting the ladies in choosing which items might best fit their needs. After they had checked out at the cash register I could offer my assistance in carrying their groceries to their car for them. Having more quality time to spend with them would allow me to enter into more interesting conversations. Discussing perhaps the more intimate facets of the weather. Or showing sympathy for their time being spent bored and lonely on a rainydays for shopping. Creating suggestions for more interesting and fun ways one might find to fill their day.

It didn't take very long at all before I got my first response. She was a 39-year-old housewife of a retired service man that traveled a lot and left her lonely too long at a time. As it turned out she was a prime candidate to fill my every need. I guess living from base to base in those days when the key clubs were just getting started helped fulfill her qualifications to be my sexual librarian. Complete with the needs and desires along with no feelings of guilt, we embarked on a very beneficial but undercover relationship. Some people refer to them as backstreet affairs. As far as I was concerned this was to be a total exploratory and learning process for me. She was a woman, loving her for that reason alone was enough for me. We both discussed and had the understanding from the start that heart-felt emotions must not play a part.

The only problem with that was it was new territory for me and I was being led by a pro. She was taking me places I had never been, teaching me things I didn't know was possible. It took me about one hour and a half to fall head over heels in love with her. I had fallen into a love pot and never wanted to leave. I just wanted to live there full time and keep cooking until the pot boiled over the relationship had gone along nicely for about three months. She was an excellent teacher. I guess I was an okay student. There were only a couple maneuvers that she had to instruct me on more than once.

One day we were very deeply involved in pleasing our desires when she got a phone call from her husband. He got back from his trip a day early and stopped by his office to give her a call while they were unloading his truck. He was a big man. I weighed maybe 140 pounds, he weighed probably 250 and was an expert marksman in the service. I had only shot a gun maybe twice in my life. And he was about to catch me with his wife. All these crazy, I don't want to die, thoughts were running through my head while she was helping me get out of bed. It only took me about 30 seconds to decide what was more important to me, my life or her pussy. I left so fast

I forgot to say goodbye and thank you, so I'm saying it now. There always seemed to be a JoAnn everywhere at the right time in my life. Assisting and allowing me to acquire the knowledge necessary so that I might achieve the point of excellence in performing the many different stages of being respectful to the needs and feelings of my partners during the process of fulfilling the obligations to the art of making love. For example, the responsibility of providing sensual, sexual stimulation while in the process of performing top-notch excitement for the enticement of an ecstasy filled orgasmic response to that aforementioned art. One they would not soon forget. If they shared my enthusiasm for memories, it would take them longer than a lifetime to forget.

For my next experience I made sure I had absolutely no possibility of anything thing happening that might be hazardous to my health I was not a fan of the features running scared presented.

She had just graduated from college a couple years prior to that and was a substitute teacher for the schools in that area. As a matter of fact she had been a substitute teacher for my English class a couple days my senior year she had her own apartment and played the guitar and sang. We had a lot of fun, but I think I ended up teaching her more than she taught me. Playing the part of the teacher was very satisfying to me. I was able to accomplish precisely what I wanted to. Thanks to my former teachers I was able to leave her breathless and begging for more several times during our stretch together. Regrettably that time was cut rather short. She got a full-time teaching job in a different county and we said our goodbyes.

I had been relatively idle in relation to my favorite pastime. I guess I was going through what some people call a dry spell. Had it not been for a couple eventful evenings at one of the local beer joints I might have thought I was losing my touch. The last thing I wanted was to get rusty with my skills.

I was feeling kind of bored on one of my days off and stopped by a friend of mines gas station as some of us would do from time to time. I was sitting out front with the owner and a couple other guys that had been playing cards in the back room. A car pulled up across the street at the courthouse that I had never seen before so I paid particular attention to who was driving. She got out of the car and stood up, my tongue immediately got hard and my dick was trying to get out of my skivvies. I couldn't talk and I couldn't walk, all I could do was think about how gorgeous she was and how well she was wearing those skin-tight white slacks. I told one of the guys that I had to find out who the hell she was he said, "Man you are getting all the pussy in town anyway, why don't you save some for somebody else. If you had to get an operation on your head all they would find in there is a bunch of little pussy's. Besides, if you get into that you're going to die. I know her husband and he will shoot your ass. He married her when he got out of the Army and he is damn proud of her." I ask him who he was and he told me but it didn't make any difference I was already loving her in my mind.

I waited for her to come out of the courthouse and get in her car. As she started backing out from her parking space I got up and walked, hard on and all, out and leaned up against one of the gas pumps. That put me closer to the road and right in her line of vision. When she drove by I knew she had to see me so I smiled and gave her a nice friendly wave with my hand and my prick.

I figured there was no better time than the present to get this process started. With total disregard for life and limb I began walking over to my car. The guy I had been talking to about her shouted out, "You pussy crazy son-of-a-bitch! I'm serious man, you're about to lose your head over a little piece of ass." I got into my car and started it up, looked over at him smiled and said, "I can't help myself man I got this empty feeling in my head and it's just enough room for one more pussy. I've got that "ole" mind over matter thing going on too. She's on my mind and nothing else matters, see you later." He yelled back at me, "Maybe, if you're lucky."

I followed her from a distance to the local dentist office. She pulled into the parking lot and parked. I thought maybe she had an appointment and prepared myself to be patiently waiting for her to return. Time went by and a couple of people came and went. This kind of let me know she must be having a special procedure done if it's taking this long.

I thought I would just go in and pretend to want to make an appointment. As I opened the door and walked in, there she was, sitting at the receptionist desk. She looked up at me, smiled and said, "May I help you?" It happened again. I immediately turned and went back out the door. It's a little difficult to walk with a hard-on when you're wearing tight jeans. And almost impossible to speak when your tongue is stiffly tied.

I knew I had to come up with some way to overcome this affect she was having on me so that I might regain my ability to penetrate her defense mechanism. I also had to come up with a good enough excuse to be able to talk to her without biting my tongue. It wasn't going to be the easiest thing I'd ever done, and why was I doing it. So I could possibly get shot.

I decided I would drive around for a few minutes to clear my head. Maybe in the process it would give my tongue and my cock a chance to reclaim normal status and have a neutral affect on my mind. Suddenly I had an idea. I remembered my senior year in high school I had to buy a new jockstrap for physical education class. I drove to my house, said hello to my aunt, got a glass of milk and went to my room. Sat the milk on the dresser and started looking for my jockstrap. When I found it I drank half the glass of milk and went over and laid down on the bed. There, with the help of the ceiling, I began to prepare a plan of action that I would hopefully be able to execute.

After resting my eyes a few minutes I got up and drank the rest of my milk. I have always loved milk. Seems like every time I taste it I have flashbacks to the nipple filled with moma's milk. I went into the bathroom to wash up, brush my teeth and put on my jockstrap. The rest of my plan kind of fell into place. I put a piece of juicy fruit chewing gum in my mouth to hopefully help occupy my tongue and keep my breath fresh.

Very soon I arrived at my destination. Having full intentions of making an appointment, I opened the door and walked in. Once again I received the same greeting. This time my response was considerably more controlled. Though I could feel strange little twitches in both problem areas I was quite capable of walking over to the desk.

While chewing rather vigorously I managed to tell her I would like to make an appointment. It was getting to be later in the day and I guess all the appointments had been filled because no-one was in the reception area. This made it better for me. It allowed me to be able to talk more freely without worrying so much about my tongue problem.

I told her I'd had a toothache for a couple days and wanted to find out what the problem was. She made an appointment for me and handed me a card with the date and time on it along with a little plaster cast statue of Dick Tracy. I guess I looked a little puzzled, so she told me. "The doctor said I should give one of these to each little boy that comes into the office." I said, "Well, thank you very much. I am honored that you put me in that category, and I shall treasure this statue forever. I wonder if I could get you to do me a favor and write your name on this card. That way I won't forget who to ask for when I call. Not that I could forget you, but you know little boys sometimes do forget."

Her response was receptive and we were both smiling at our kidding conversation. She handed the card back to me with her name on it and said, "Don't forget we close at five." I glanced at the card and replied, "Why Andrea, thank you I will try hard not to forget. Andrea, what a pretty name my dear. It is so very becoming to you."

She accepted the complement without response. I found the door-knob and regretfully made my exit. When I got back to the car I put the card and the statue in a little tray for safekeeping.

With my late afternoon primary goal accomplished, I thought I would drive back by the gas station to shoot the breeze a little more. As I pulled in and parked I noticed the party I had been talking with before leaning over saying something to the person that was beside him. Not that I really gave the shit what they were talking about, but I soon found out it had been about me.

I suppose since this particular gas station was known in town for its gambling procedures and under market numbers, they couldn't help but taking bets on me and giving odds as to how long I'd live. The odds-maker, who was the owner of the gas station, pretty much had it all covered. He put the odds of me meeting at her that day at 4 to 1. The odds of me getting her name at 5 to 1 The odds of me getting her name and phone number at 10 to 1, and her work number was not to be considered. The odds of us actually having an affair were at 50 to 1. And if any of the above 4 events took place he put the odds against me living more than 30 days at 100 to 1.

After they had related to me the betting procedures they had arranged I asked them how in the hell they thought they were going to find out if any of those aforementioned odds were met. The odds-maker said to me. "Son, a man's dick has a mind of its own without a conscience and is very proud of its accomplishments. If you have a damn brain in your head, you will put a zipper on your mouth and keep your cock under lock-an-key. Otherwise, all bets will be paid at your funeral."

I didn't give it a second thought. Mainly because, I don't normally run around telling everyone who I'm sleeping with. I just never thought that was a very smart thing to do. Especially when 98% of your rendezvous's involve someone else's spouse, fiancé, or girlfriend. If not for respect of your life, out of respect for them, it deserves privacy.

There was a considerable amount of excitement with completing the placing of their bets along with the possibility of their making a little extra money if I were to be successful. A couple of them seemed to be a little more excited over the possibility of making more if I were to be the recipient of the husband's wrath. I really wasn't quite sure what to think about that. However, the possibility of them making any money at all on me as far as I was concerned was not going to happen.

I was the kind of person that took mental notes and wrote memoirs for later life disclosures. I had always been quite content with knowing whatever and with whom I was involved with had been a pleasing and learning experience for both parties. It was very important to me to please my partner and learn whatever I could

The next day I arranged to switch shifts on my job. Two of us usually cover the afternoon and evening shifts from 1:00 p.m. to 9:00 pm every other week. I had covered it last week and unfortunately would not be working in the evening this week. I decided to try making myself available just in case Andrea would be doing any grocery shopping. I knew it was more likely she would be shopping in the evening than in the morning since she was working all day.

As it turned out I had to wait a couple days for my dream to come true. I was busying myself with the produce displays whistling my way through the afternoon. Suddenly my mental faculties were sidetracked by an aroma I had become familiar with at the dentist office.

Without turning around I proclaimed, "What an overwhelmingly pleasurable aroma to take the place of lettuce and broccoli. It almost smells too good to eat." I knew it had to be her.

As I turned around she said, "I'm sorry, is it too much?" I replied, "My dear Andrea, it is absolutely perfectly wonderful and should only be worn by someone as lovely as you. As you came close enough to infiltrate my senses that wonderful aroma told me I had a dream coming true. And that dream Andrea, was you."

She responded with, "Man you sure lay it on thick. It sounds like you got that straight out of a Casanova, or a Don Won love story. Perhaps you read too much. Maybe you wouldn't have dreams like that if you didn't read so much."

I said, "'Tis you my dear I read, you are the book that plants the seed; to form the dream for which I need, allowing you to comfort me; where all your beauty I can see. While bringing pleasure to my work, my duty, I fear I must not shirk; I cannot fail to let you know, dear-dear Andrea, how you set my heart aglow." She looked a little stunned, maybe she was taking it all in and letting it settle. She walked away without responding.

I went on refreshing the look of the produce department. Once I had finished that I moved into the shelf stalking part of my evening. That part of my job was the boring part. But I had learned if I count the cans the small boxes and loaves of bread and pretend I was building something it made the time pass faster. I of course, was building a mental safe haven where Andrea and I could meet secretly without fear of being discovered, if that time ever came.

I suppose it had been probably 5 minutes maybe 10, when my sense of smell began once more to fill all my other senses with desires of lust for Andrea. She walked up to me and said, "I'm sorry, I just had to walk away. I have never had anyone speak to me with your kind of flavor. I guess it took me by surprise and I didn't know what to say. Especially, since I am a married woman." I responded to her by saying, "My dear deliriously delectable young lady, I knew you were married. But that didn't matter to me. With no disrespect to your husband or to you, we are all born with different ideas about love, life, and the sacred sanctions marriage holds over us. I am not one to be bound by such sanctions. I am what I am, and I will do and say the things I want to. It seems I felt I would be guilty of an unforgivable sin if I were not to bestow upon one so beautiful my innermost thoughts of her and how she wore her beauty."

Once again she walked away without saying anything. Possibly I had given her no choice. However, one thing I did find out was that her husband was obviously not known for his loving remarks. That is always helpful, it leaves the door to her heart unlocked and willing to open under the right circumstances. As I watched her walk away, it became quite obviously necessary for her to exit quickly. And so she did without purchasing anything.

Time went by very slowly for the next two days. Then surprisingly, on Saturday afternoon about 2 o'clock there she was. As she approached the produce department she had picked up a few items on the way so I felt reasonably sure that she was going to shop a little today. She came closer and I said, "Hey pretty lady, I am glad to see you back. My heart has been filled with sadness not knowing if I would ever see you again." She responded with, "Who are you, and where do you come from? Do you stay up all night thinking about these things and what to say? I don't know how much more of this I can take."

I replied, "First question first, I my dear am a figment of your imagination living in your subconscious mind. I am trying to make my way inside your heart. Yes, you are on my mind constantly day and night. Supplying me with what I should say, and helping me practice how to say it. If you wish, I will cease. Though it would cause me much sorrow I do not wish for you to be uncomfortable. That being the case, I am sure you will let me know tonight in dreams of you."

And so it was. That night after work I went home after a couple beers and a shot of Jack with the guys at the gas station. I got out my pen and paper pad and began to write a dream. I wrote it exactly the way I wanted it to play out. Then I turned out the lights and went to bed and fell immediately into dreamland. The next day was Sunday and I didn't have to work. I took a long drive in the country and stopped at several wide spots in the road to write a line or two that had been conveyed to me through my dreams. In dreamland, for a true dreamer, dreams work out the way you want. I have been by many people considered a dreamer, so I had very little problem with working out my dreams. Now it was all left for me to make them come true.

Surviving Sunday seemed like the simplest thing I had to do. Then all of a sudden it was Monday and I was scheduled to work from 1 to 9 PM. As I began to structure the produce display to a state of attractiveness I was greeted by the ultimate supreme surprise. There was Andrea, with her gorgeous display of woman. Her beauty in person caused paling by comparison for my dreams of her. I never thought that to be possible. Andrea had worked the impossible in my mind so many time's. This was just one more.

As our eyes met, I projected a look of shock. And she asked, "Are you alright?" I replied, almost stuttering, "Yes I am, as a matter of fact I'm perfect, thanks to you." She inquired, "What do you mean, how have I manufactured your perfection?" I said, "You are so pleasing to the eye and so easy on the mind. It could probably be considered a crime the effect your body, your beauty, and the way you wear your clothes have on me. How did you know to wear that dress? You make it look so pretty, you should be a model. You are bringing to life a vision I had of you in the early-early hours of Sunday morning in my dreams. You wore that same lovely dress, oh my dear Andrea, how you illuminate its flower structure with your beauty and that sensually sexy smile that serves up a tray of tantalizing temptation. It could transform the mind of any man partaking into one of a sensualist."

I reached over to the flower section and snipped off a single short stemmed pink rose, turned to Andrea and placed it in her hair, then proclaimed, "You do not need this, but I feel I must contribute something to your magnificence. Perhaps it's best if you go before I get fired or project my desires and addiction to sensualism by displaying my true intentions for the over indulgence of your sensuality."

With an imposingly beautiful smile and the portrayal of grandeur in a teardrop, she turned and slowly walked away. I retreated to the back room of the store where we kept supplies and the bathrooms were. I needed to clear my throat and wash my face before I attempted to assist anyone that might need my services.

It seemed like the store was getting busier. It could have been that I just really wasn't used to working that many evening shifts in a row. But the days were going by faster and that was a shift I wanted to be on to make myself accessible to Andrea if and when she would decide to make an appearance.

For the next couple weeks it seemed as though Andrea would find something she needed almost every day. It was always a great feeling when she came by. I got the distinct impression it was something she was feeling as well.

The afternoon and evening shift was fine for me. I could sleep later and I didn't have to worry about the ridiculous rhetoric that was going on at the gas station when I'd stop by. Besides I had outlived a couple of their predictions already, and certainly intended to outlive them all.

About one month had gone by since I first met Andrea. I will have to say I have never enjoyed myself more in my life than I did during that time. That gorgeous young lady preserved a prominent position of pleasurable permanence in my memory. Still to this day, from time to time I will put on a nice soothing classical album, sometimes maybe Opera and have a glass of wine, or maybe Brandy. Sometimes just a beer, while I enjoy some quality memories with Andrea on my mind.

We were far enough along with our flirtatious mannerisms and pledges of adoration that we finally set up our first rendezvous. It was to take place at the local park. Unfortunately, it had only one way in and one way out. Now you know how unconsciously in love with love I was at the time.

It turned out fine, the togetherness was fantabulous, but I never pinned myself in again. One thing my father, my uncle, and another older and good friend always told me. Never get yourself into a situation you cannot get out of. It would have been a perfect place for a jealous husband to have performed an execution. Thank "God" that did not happen.

We pulled up and parked side-by-side. I got out first and opened my truck. Andrea got out and asked what I was doing. I told her I was getting a cooler with a few drinks in it, a blanket and a couple pillows. She smiled but had an unusual look on her face and asked. "Do you always carry these articles in your trunk?" I closed the trunk and laid everything on top of it, turned to her and said. "You gorgeous creature, I could never forgive myself if I were to ask you to sit with me in the uncomfortable confines of a car. Or spend our special time together on the hard bench seats of the picnic table. Much less, ask you to place that very voluptuous body on the ground without a cover." Together we laid the blanket down and placed the pillows. I looked at her, she looked at me. We both got stars in our eyes and fell into each other's arms. It was like a spontaneous combustion, or an explosion. It might be equated to starting a fire by pouring too much gasoline on it. We were both steaming and had absolutely no problem going the places we needed to go. Fortunately for us the park was deserted. This made things much easier to carry out the exploratory process of each other's body.

I didn't have any idea what she thought of my body. All I know was she had no problem at all finding a nipple to suck an kiss, or a bellybutton to play with while gently massaging and stroking the area surrounding my overly anxious and partially slow drip-drooling-dick. We both had totally stripped naked. I have no idea what we would have done had somebody driven into the park. We could have cared less and was not even thinking about it.

This event was such an overdue desire I seemed to be drooling all over the place but I was trying very hard not to pop a nut. I sat back and visually took a picture of every fraction of an inch of her body, including rolling her over and kiss-licking her butt crack. She was absolutely perfect, not one thing with a hint of misplacement. "God" she was so gorgeously scrumptious, too pretty to touch and much too precious to eat. I just sat there gazing at what was about to become my grazing grounds. I wanted to tongue travel every little teeny tiny crevice. And so the animalistic characteristics of my soul began to surface. From her forehead while running my fingers through her beautiful blonde hair, to the tip of her toes while gently massaging her clitoris and teasingly titillating her twat. I gave her a little nudge and she assisted me by rolling over on her tummy. I continued my tongue washing of her entire body as I finger reamed and prickingly-praise-prepped her perfect little prune for the possibility of a surprise later.

Through the entire tongue washing process she held on to my staff, steadily stroking slowly. She had noticed I was drooling and occasionally would change hands to lick off the secretions of come want-to-be's. My clock was as hard as a rock and suddenly it seemed somewhat larger than ever before. I think it was probably because it was about to blow. Andrea realized it and started to make a move to orally gratify my prick. I did not want to prematurely ejaculate. But there was absolutely nothing I could do when the lips of that gorgeous face touched the head of my cock she was the recipient of a load that would have choked a normal lady. But Andrea was so far above the norm it didn't even faze her. I thought it might blow off the back of her head. Instead she swallowed it like it was a delicious milkshake and kept sucking until I was completely empty from love juices.

Without saying a word Andrea pushed me backward and laid claim to the top side position by spreading her pussy lips with the fingers on one hand while directing my cock into her love nest with the other. After navigating about halfway in and around the vagina sheath, or her vaginal membrane, there was nothing I could do but come. I went off like a repeating rifle and she jammed it all the way in and started rocking topside. She leaned forward to kiss me and we rolled over on her back. Almost immediately after climbing into that position she rolled partially on her right side and lifted her left leg over my right shoulder. I could feel the bottom of her pussy rubbing against the head of my cock trying to block it from getting deeper penetration. She screamed, "Yes-yes-yes, deeper, get dee-per and dee-per. I popped another nut and could feel it bouncing off the bottom of her inner pussy-wall lining. The extremely robust orgasmic sanctions failed to subdue the cock and pussy pleasures. Instead, it served as a booster and initiated the beginning of right-down-raw nitty-gritty to the bone bumping and grinding, including our hiney. No holes were barred for this lovemaking session. All openings seem to have signs saying, "Available, please enter as often and forceful as possible, thank you." Of course they would be signed, *(bodily orifices!!!)* What else did you expect?

The very successful event supplied one lust filled surprise after another. Almost continuous coming on both parts. So many I couldn't count, didn't want to, and wasn't trying. It lasted about an hour and a half. As we were leaving the park Andrea let me know just how happy she was. She gifted me with a long-lasting and very wet lip- lock that delivered a tasty serving of sexual secretions with her tongue. Not only did that make me very happy it also told me a couple things. Andrea was a very desirably beautiful and sexy young lady. She was a great lover who had been left love hungry, perhaps on the verge of starvation for much too long. I made up my mind that if I could help it that would certainly be one problem she would never have again as long as I knew her. I was unaware of how her husband treated her or how they got along. I can only give account of the pleasures she introduced me to through her wonderfully wavering womanly ways.

When I left the park, I went straight to my house and put on some nice soothing music. I felt the need to slow my mind down a bit before starting to make selections for a safe haven where Andrea and I could have our next get-together.

I had laid down on my bed to rest a little and think a lot. Unfortunately, I fell asleep and did very little thinking. It was probably best to give it a couple days so I could come up with more choices for our next rendezvous.

I was still working the late shift but for some strange reason had a three day break in my scheduling. It became more and more difficult each day not to call Andrea at work. Managing it the best I could I occupied my time by going to visit my mother and some of my other relatives.

Eventually the three days past and I was at work. I never thought I'd be that happy to be on the job. Nothing had changed it was just a scheduling problem. So back to doing the same old thing, beautifying the produce displays.

I heard someone behind me and looked up above the display case to the mirror, it was Andrea. She was kind of nonchalantly looking around at different things in the produce section and whispered to me. "Where have you been? I have been here every day since I saw you. I started thinking maybe you left town." Without turning around so it wouldn't look so obvious we were having a conversation, I replied. "For some strange reason I was not on the schedule. We probably shouldn't talk too much today. I'd have to be crazy to leave town, and I'm not crazy yet." She glanced up at me in the mirror and I whispered. **"You were fantastic!!! I am about to have an _orgasm_ just looking at you bye-bye baby, see you tomorrow or next day." She mimicked a kiss back to me without a smile, then suddenly moved _her sexy lips and mouth_ to say. You too, okay."**

As she moved on along, picking up an item here and there, I wondered if her house was getting overstocked with groceries. What were my coworkers thinking. Especially the one cashier. Her name was Lola. She was very flirtatious and had been known to have several affairs. Providing her with personal knowledge of how these things work I would have been very surprised if she wasn't a little suspicious, and knew she'd let me know before long.

Things were moving along very well. Andrea and I saw each other several times over the next couple months. Maybe not as many times as I would've liked. But at least the times we met were extremely satisfying and very safe.

I had spent very little time stopping by the gas station to listen to all the bull-shit that was going around. As long as it wasn't involving me I could care less. Though I will have to say, how they found out some of the things they found out I'll never know, but most of the time it turned out to be true.

I was coming up on my first year anniversary at work and was due for a one-week vacation. I met with Andrea in a nearby town where I knew it would be safe and told her I would be gone for a week. She wasn't happy, nor was I. it would have been much more satisfying staying around her and trying to arrange times, places, and meetings. But for reasons which I have no explanation, I chose to take a vacation in the comforts provided by the capital city of this great country, Washington DC.

CHAPTER 4

Nymphomania Lover

Not only was I amazed and somewhat comforted by the national monuments and all the history they revealed, but I was absolutely totally excited by the possibilities provided for sexual pleasures. It just seemed like everywhere I went there were government secretaries waiting to be awed by some flirtatious male who had no way of coping except overloading his ass with his verbal deliveries.

Some friends of mine had gone to DC straight from high school to work for the government. I got in touch with a few of them, ones that I felt I could trust. One in particular who I knew would screw over you in a heartbeat but he was honest. He got me an invitation to a party, and man, it was over. I fell in love with that city. It had young ladies from every state in the United States and every country in the world. It felt like my prick and my mind had a magnet attached and it was drawing me to be there. The girls/young ladies were beautiful and they were dressed for the occasion. It was like they were looking for what I was looking for and advertised it with every move and expression.

It took about 15 minutes to decide who was going home with me, or whom I would be going home with. Unfortunately, it was the same young lady that my friend had been trying to make a memory with. Though he wasn't really pleased, I convinced him if he allowed me to tread water first I would put in a good word for him. We knew each other from school, he was one of my classmates. I believe he realized that when I made up my mind that's how it was going to be. So, she went home with me, or actually I went to her home.

DC's a wonderful place, home could be anything from a one room efficiency apartment to a 15-bedroom house. She had the first of the aforementioned. As my mind allows me to take a trip back in time and wade through the cobwebs so that I might right this ship, her name was Sandy, and she was just like a piece of candy. So sweet and ready-to-eat and holding on with both hands to my meat. We barely made it through her apartment door until we found our way to the floor. From that point on there was nothing to do except hold each other tight and fucking screw. And screw we did, in every way possible. She seemed just like the female side of me. In her mind she lived for what I wanted to be doing throughout eternity, making love. So, we fucking made love for several hours, but it only seemed like minutes. Then we showered and fucked some more. Sandy loved to fuck, and regardless of position I just could not get deep enough to satisfy her lust. It seemed like she enjoyed the pain of my prick with its pound-slapping-pressure trying hard to penetrate her pussy wall. It was either that or she loved to scream.

My hotel was only about a block and a half from her apartment and it was Sunday with no restrictions on street parking. So guess what, we continued on our quest to outdo each other between the covers. Needless to say there were no losers. How could there be a loser when both of us were full of the same lust filled sexual desires and possessed an insatiable appetite for sexual pleasures.

It seems the losers were determined by hunger pains on both our parts. One could hear and occasional tummy rumble. After a few more of those from both of us, at almost precise same time we looked at each other and asked, "Are you hungry?" Without either of us admitting defeat, we reached out for each other's hands and together became quite accomplished in taking a very pronounced, overflowing with sexual activities joint shower, in a smaller than average bathtub.

It had been a very pleasantly productive first day on my trip to what would become my future home, the Washington metropolitan area. By the time we walked out the door to be on our way to get something to eat it was about 5:30 in the evening.

We found a little Mexican restaurant a few blocks away. It was almost right in the heart of the section of DC that was referred to as Georgetown. I wasn't into Mexican food that much, but Sandy indicated that she had been there and it was a really nice place. She said, "They have these roving minstrels and later in the evening a floor show. The atmosphere is great and besides that the foods good." And that was the end of that.

Most of the time in my life, the young lady was always right. It was no different this time, the food was good. They had a waiter who carried a squeezable jug of wine. It looked like a leather bag with a pointed spout. He could squeeze the bag and hit your mouth from across the table without spilling a drop. I guess that's part of the floor show or the atmosphere Sandy was talking about. However I would have preferred he used a beer.

Sandy seemed to enjoy watching all these different little things that was going on while I spent more of my time trying to figure out what I was eating. Though I will say it was very tasty.

After dinner and a few drinks, we took a little walk through Georgetown. It seemed to have a nightclub to suit whatever kind of music you desired. About 9:30 we decided to head back home and I hailed a cab. That was probably the smartest thing for me to do because we got all wrapped up in the backseat of the taxi. Fortunately, I had already given the address of our destination to the cabbie. I suppose when he realized what was going on he just decided to keep the meter running and chose not to disturb us.

That was my first experience with taxicab seduction, but not my last Sandy was such a sweetheart, displaying her manners of appreciation by bestowing upon me a very soothing ball licking blow job. I think the cabbie was pounding his prong. He kind of stuttered a little bit when he gave me the charges. I paid him and gave him a $10 tip and said. "Thanks man!" He replied, "No problem, call me anytime you need a personal chauffeur." And handed me his card.

It was almost 11 PM and Sandy had already decided to take sick leave for the next day. So I figured the best thing I could do would be find a legal parking space to get rid of the morning rush-hour restrictions. I asked Sandy if she wanted to go with me to find a parking space. She shook her head yes and we started the almost impossible journey of finding a legal parking place at that time on Sunday night. Finally, I drove to my motel parking garage and showed them my room key free guest parking was included in my room charges.

That gave us a few minutes to talk a little and enjoy the scenery along with each other's company. We actually had to walk past the front of the White House. There didn't seem to be anything going on there. I remember thinking to myself that it would be nice to see Jackie, of course, knowing that was just a lot of wishful thinking.

It must've been midnight by the time we got back to Sandy's apartment. She turned on some music and said, "Relax a minute, I'll get some things and be back soon." I thought she was going to put her nightgown or robe on so I didn't think much about it. In a few minutes she rolled out this little tray on wheels with a lot of, what turned out later to be love toys and added attractions. Such as peanut butter and jelly, cool whip, honey, a cucumber, a carrot, and about a 12 to 15 inch straight roll of pepperoni. I guess she wanted something to munch on, so I asked, "What's all this?" She just smiled and said, "Give me a couple more minutes and you'll see." Then with a certain questionable sexy look to go along with that smile Sandy glanced back at me and said, "Surely you're not trying to tell me you're not hungry."

Sure enough, just like she promised, Sandy rolled out two more trays. One was occupied by a rather large platter with ice covering the bottom. Sitting on the ice were two bowls. One filled with strawberries, the other filled with cherries. The other tray held what appeared to be a tiny little refrigerator or freezer. Inside was a bowl of ice cubes and another bowl of cherry vanilla swirl ice cream. Sitting on the outside of that same tray was a medium-size bottle of vegetable oil, a bottle of chocolate syrup and a somewhat smaller bottle of olive oil. She took the Olive oil and put it into the freezer, or should I say ice box. Little did I know at the time, the term icebox might be applicable to one of the games we would be playing later.

After the completion of Sandy's surprising 10 course snack prep work, she put the finishing touches on it by pulling the couch out into a bed. And with pains taking efforts of perfection, straightening the sheets and fluffing the pillows. Sandy sat down on my lap and asked, "What do you think?" I replied, "It's your show baby. I am just your supporting actor. Whatever you tell me to do, your wish shall be my command. It sure looks interesting."

By this time, I had figured out there was a method to her madness. I also had a feeling I was going to be playing an intricate part in methodizing her madness. She leaned over and gave me little kiss on the cheek and whispered, "Don't go anywhere, I'll be right back."

I don't know where the hell she thought I was going. I was not about to go anywhere. I was too damned interested in playing whatever parts she wanted me to play in the unfolding of this mystery. Hell, I was so far into this game even my toes were hard.

In about 10 minutes Sandy made a very sexy appearance at the opening of what you might call the living room, or bedroom. She was wearing a knee length see-through titty pink négligée. Along with what looked like 6 or 7 inch stiletto heeled shoes of matching color.

On her face Sandy wore a smile of temptation. With one hand at her lips, while kiss-sucking a juicy strawberry. She used the other hand to tantalize me by dangling a cherry on a stem in the direction of my mouth. Then Sandy took three modeling strut-steps and her bellybutton was staring me in the eyes. I put my arms around her and buried my face in her sexy-see-through négligée while molesting her tummy with a mouth massage. I laid her down gently on the bed and together we kiss-suckingly devoured what remained of Sandy's strawberry. I looked down at her and said very emphatically, "**Baby you are Bad! Bad! Bad!!! I don't know what you're up to, but I know where my mind is. Give me that damn cherry, I'm going to introduce it to its new home.**" When I open my mouth, she put the cherry inside and pulled the stem off. Needless to say the cherry went swimming, and I of course, went on a successful deep-pussy tongue-diving rescue mission.

And so the games began. Once I retrieve the cherry, we held another celebratory duel-munching session. And it was on, our minds were in sync we were thinking as one. I figured it was all by Sandy's design so I would give her the honors of taking the lead.

CHAPTER 5

Talented Tongue Travel

S andy began by providing me with a total body tantalizing tongue treatment. She was a very talented lovemaking machine, especially for being so young. Sandy used her tongue much like a blind person would use their fingers to feel their way around and recognize certain parts of the face or body. She really knew how to maneuver her tongue and mess with your mind.

It was satisfyingly soothing, sensationally sensual and tormentingly sexy. She made it feel like her tongue had three or four little fingers at its point. Sandy had provided me with a heavenly hard-on. When she got to that part of my body it felt like I was losing mental control because of the torturing taunts of trickery provided by her talented tongue. Sandy's tongue trailed the head of my cock and tongue slapped it hard twice while it seemed like at the same time she was nibble-nip-sucking the tiny opening in the head of my penis. Never slowing, always blowing and performing a vibrating tongue tap-dance up and down the entirety of my cock/shaft several times with a sensational salivating nut sack sucking massage rolling both balls around from jaw to jaw with her tongue performing a soft lip-lock biting kiss for ball pleasing, and then again, and again. I tried to function but wasn't permitted. I was a victim of her desires. Sandy's talents were on display and I was totally impressed. I was conscious only to the sensation her sexual desires brought to life in my body. The only thoughts that went through my mind were of the wonders of lovemaking. I think I entertained the idea of living my entire life in that very position with Sandy forever.

She partially rose to her knees, and for my viewing pleasure's, took her time spreading her pussy-lips with her fingers and serving herself a short soft inner pussy-wall massage. I was busting nut after nut. Sandy scooped them up with the other hand and ravishingly licked them off as though she was starving for come. She opened her pussy lips a little wider and did two, maybe three entrances and exits providing a teasingly tormenting taste of her talents to my hungry for her love nest cock. She mastered swallowing another major mouth-full of my mother loads without choking. Then she pulled off and I shot all over her belly. She was wiping, licking, and rubbing it all over us. Sandy continued to provide me with these pleasures for at least the next hour or two. My mental was in no condition to understand time. All I knew and cared about was that our time was being orgasmicly blessed by love juices from both of us. Sandy had also provided me with excitement enough to quickly recover from being too much of a fast shooter. It appeared to make her happy that I was so quick on the trigger. She worked diligently to make me come time after time and said, "That is so cool, I hope you have an endless supply of come. I want all the come-juice you can pleasure me with, that's where I get my energy. **So, baby come-come-come-baby come!!!**" Sandy grabbed my cock faster than fast and immediately started pounding my pecker with rapid fire rhythm and I shot three or four more times. She just pointed my prick towards her face and was spreading it around as though she were putting on lotion. I was trying to hold my own in this lovemaking matinee, but I was having a hard time keeping up with her. She had already turned my prick into a peanut butter and jelly belly-rolled-popsicle, and backed that up with a solution of cool whip over the honey on my nuts. All I had been able to achieve was deliver a mouth full of cherry vanilla swirl ice cream with a little chocolate syrup by mouth to her pussy. Sandy's pussy was so hot the ice cream was melting as soon as it made contact. Her pussy hairs were straining it on the way back to my mouth. I was hoping not to choke because I didn't want it to seem like I didn't know what I was doing. I guess it was so obvious that I fucking did not know what I was doing Sandy started laughing. Which provided a split-second hesitation in the action and I said, "It's not funny damn-it, I don't know how to pack your pussy. You got a hot box baby and its melting the ice cream before I can push it in with my tongue, maybe I should try using a spoon." She broke the laughter a little, and said, "Use your fingers and hands for inserting it and mouth and tongue for recovering the tasty smoldering juices, no spoon necessary. The spoon was to be used to mix the peanut butter and jelly." I replied, "Your pussy is so hot. Why do you have such a hot box?" She said, "It's my nature, I'm just naturally hot. Cool it down, there's a bowl of ice cubes, they'll do the trick. I like ice cube sex, it's a lot of fun.

Have you ever drank pussy ice water?" I replied, "No, but I think I'm going to try it right now." And that's exactly what I did. I had a nice soothing drink of peanut butter and jelly mixed with Cool Whip and honey flavored, watered-down pussy juice.

I didn't want to seem like I was embarrassed, why in the hell couldn't I have thought of that. Sandy was just so much better prepared and experienced than I was. But she didn't care. She liked playing the role of teacher I think she got off watching her partner try to keep up with her ability to make love. It probably played a part in why she was so hot all the time. Every part of her body was overheated, not just her pussy.

I couldn't help but think, where the hell did she come from? Where was she when I needed her at age 5,6,7. Or for that matter, any of my adolescent years. It would have been nice to have been that prepared back then. I could have been providing so much more pleasure for my partners all these years if I had known Sandy then. I have to ask her some questions. I've got to know more about her past and how she got to where she is with her knowledge of sex and the stimulating process of how she makes love.

I grabbed an opportunity to call a quick timeout. I was hoping she would understand where I was coming from. I said, "Sandy my dear, it is so obvious I am totally outclassed when it comes to your lovemaking ability. Not that I want to be better than you, but I want to make you feel as good as you make me feel. If you could find it in your heart to let that gorgeous face and your beautiful body do me a favor, please teach me everything you know. You want all the come juices I have. I'll trade you, all the orgasmic explosions and drooling juices you want for all the knowledge you have. She smiled and said, "It's a deal, let's seal it with a kiss instead of a handshake."

We kissed and just laid back on the bed while finger- walking each other's bodies, acknowledgment of where the both of us were coming from became obvious. Every now and then she would put a couple strokes on my sticky peanut butter jelly prick. I would return the gesture with either a gentle touch to her clit or a kiss-sucking maneuver on her titty-nipple.

After a few minutes of talking through these things we had experienced while growing from a child, it seemed like we were one of the same. Sandy was always getting into trouble from the unusual actions and desires she displayed while playing games with little boys. Much the same as I did, while enjoying the company of little girls.

I think the reason she was so much more advanced than I, was because she knew she could learn by reading as well as doing. Every time she could find any kind of article having to do with a woman's body or sexual maneuvers, she would read it. I never wanted to read about it, I wanted to explore it so I could write about it. Now I find myself lacking knowledge of an area that I am totally, and always have been, in love with.

We must have been born under the same sign at the exact same time for I was just like Sandy told me she was. I wanted the same things she wanted. Could it be we were cosmic-twins.

Sandy told me she knew at a very young age that she liked fucking and sex any way it could happen. She couldn't wait to graduate from high school so she could leave home and live her life the way she wanted to. I can tell you she lives and wears her desires very well. Sandy is also extremely pleasing to a little country-cunt-licker. As I hope to be some day for a little lady, big-city cock-sucker. Sandy also told me not to be afraid to try anything with her. She said, "I love sex, any-way, any place, and any time. If you have questions, ask me. Do not worry about hurting me. Do or try to do anything you wish. I will tell you if it hurts." Some people, I am sure, think I am a slut. I might perform three or four different acts of sex with three or four different partners, at any event I were to attend. Whether it be a party, movie, dance, ballgame, or dinner. It is just something I love to do. I have an undying desire to be involved in some sexual activity every waking moment of my life.

She explained further, "I loved to fuck so much that one of the first things I did when coming to DC was to have an operation to prevent me from getting pregnant." While making hand gestures and physically proclaiming, she said to fuck, to suck, or to play sex games. To help you pack my pussy with ice, or ice cream, or maybe just your prick, brings ultimate satisfaction to my sexual desires. I have been the recipient of many very, very intense climaxes from assisting in those type maneuvers. I have been told several times that I had nymphomania traits, and I would probably have by-sexual tendencies. Brent honey, nobody had to tell me that. The first time I made love to a girl was with my best friend. We were in the eighth grade, and man, we tore it up in the girls-restroom. We got caught and reported to the principal. They sent us home and called our parents. We didn't care, it was great and a many time reoccurring experience. We would help each other out through our high school years when there were no boys available. We loved and taught each other every possible way to have an orgasm. I still stay in touch with her. We were so good together, and I miss her. I would get with her in a heartbeat if she were to come to this area."

We had a glass of wine. I kissed her on the fore-head and said, "Sandy, you are a very special person." She said, "Well thank you Brent, I think you're okay too." I stood up and she asked, "Where are you going?" I informed her that I needed to go to the bathroom I had to pee. She very quickly jumped up and ask if she could come with me. I said, "Why sure, you know you are welcome anywhere with me. I don't imagine it's going to be too exciting for you." She proclaimed, "Oh but Brent, you can't be sure of that. I am a professional pecker holder. I love to hold a man's cock when he's peeing. I like to feel the vibration on my fingers of the stream flowing through his main vein, it turns me on." I had never heard that before, but it certainly was not going to be a problem for me or for her. Sandy could hold my cock anytime she wanted to.

CHAPTER 6

Tickle–Tickle Pee Pee

Sandy followed me into the bathroom. We were both naked, so my cock snapped to attention and saluted her. It surrendered several nervous jerky-cock moves, begging for a little **"TLC"**, while patiently awaiting Sandy's pleasures. She presented my wanting-stick of salivating love-juices with favor after favor of cock-caressing. Her fingers were perfectly positioned on my main vein so the pissing vibration would present more excitement. She got down on her knees to get as close as possible to the action. She said,

"The closer I get the better it feels. If I'm resting my boobs on my arm the vibration sometimes travels all the way to my nipples. I really like it when that happens, it's a sign of sensitivity to sexual satisfaction and keeps my mind on orgasmic bliss. In other words, it's a real turn-on." Unfortunately, there was no action. I had to piss like a race-horse. I wonder what a race-horse would do, if he had a gorgeous young lady kneeling down and holding his cock while he was trying to take a piss. I don't know about the horse, but I know I couldn't piss. Although I needed to, and wanted to, nothing would come out. It was actually starting to hurt a little bit.

The next thing Sandy taught me was one of the most important things I have learned in my life. She taught me how to piss when I couldn't. The process she used really came in handy later in life. Plus, I was also able to teach several ladies how to make it happen. Suddenly I felt her fingers tickle-walking the area from the bottom of my nut-sack and ass-hole up both butt-cheeks to the small of my back. My race-horse tendencies quickly came through with a stream that excited Sandy so much she started pleasure-moaning and slow stroking my cock. Every two or three seconds she would take her hand off and rub her fingers across her pussy-lips. Then lick them off and return to her favorite cock holding position.

Before the bathroom pleasures were complete, Sandy and I ended up doing a 69'r in the bathtub with the shower on. One of my favorite positions, if not my all-time favorite.

Once we turned the shower off, I was not sure if I had peed on her or she had peed on me. Maybe we just got into the bathtub so we could piss on each other and not know it with the shower running. All I knew for sure was that I was really glad Sandy chose me to be her plaything for a while. I was hoping it would last throughout my vacation.

While we were drying each other off I asked Sandy where she learned about the tickling procedures. She said, "I read about it in my encyclopedia of sex. Something else I read about is the reason I decided to choose you to go home with." I inquired, "What are you talking about?" She told me one of the articles that she had been reading indicated the size of a man's penis was related to the size of the veins in his hands and arms. Men with large veins tend to possess a larger than average penis. I would imagine this will be a problem, or pleasure, you will have throughout your life.

It certainly seems both predictions the article had are true in your case. I responded with, "Darn it Sandy, I thought you chose me for my looks." She replied with a smile, "That didn't hurt your chances."

(Politicians>and<Prostitutes)

These words both have the same number of letters.
They also cherish similar ways of doing business.

Screwing for top dollar!!!

Are they from the same mold???
Were they born under the same star???
Which is most honest if the truth be told???
Do we really know who they are???

Maybe they should trade places!!!

Pay this rant no mind, 'tis an excerpt of another kind; For you it was designed, not to be a waste of time; but to take your mind off the sin-filled structuring of the book you're reading now. I need a little time to rest my mind while I am gathering material to mess with yours. I will try to stay with the flow of **verbal diarrhea** one expects when you spend too much time in the **DC area.**

Government mumbo-jumbo

????????*********????????

I think I know why the government is so fucked up. I believe all the really good secretaries, much like the politicians, are sex maniacs. And they only have to work when they're not having sex. Which would be in agreement with many statistics, of that 80/20 status. 80% being sex, 20% being work. I would go farther and say the sex-a-taries probably get more accomplished during their 20% than the politicians during their 80%. This however, being a many year later after-thought, has absolutely nothing to do with my feelings of Sandy's capabilities. Whether we are talking about work, or play, I feel confident in saying that she is just as competent at her job as in her bed. I know for a fact, she carries through and completes her bedtime activities at a much greater and more pleasurable percentage level while having fun doing so, than any politician I have ever known. And I have known a few. Although, my donor ledgers might reflect that I have gifted politicians in the reverse of the aforementioned statistics. No reflections for sex-a-tarial services will be found. My favorite females are free, like politicians should be. Maybe I'm wrong but I thought taxpayer dollars paid politicians salaries. Too bad the wonderful walking, waywardly wanton women of Washington, or any other area, could not persuade Congress to pass a bill favoring their occupation as well.. This leaves me with only one logical explanation. ***Politicians are so much more like prostitutes than prostitutes are themselves.*** However, it seems to me if politicians could only consider their job serving the people as fun, they might quit trying to do their job from a horizontal position!!! This long-winded paragraph is absolutely out of place. And the results of a good bottle of brandy. Accept it for what it is, as I will, or kiss it goodbye. I know damn well it has interfered with my train of thought on this memoir of Sandy's seductively sensual, and sexually sensational, night dreams. So return with me now to those thrilling days of yesteryear when the lightning flashed and the thunder rolled and if you didn't have a woman your balls got cold.

???????***********???????

I suppose I should beg your forgiveness, piss on that. If I cannot reconstruct and circulate a memory of Sandy's expertise, hell, it will be my fault. I am only writing this damn thing. Blame it on Poe, or Michelangelo or the brandy. What's that you say, Brandy? I used to know this very special young lady named Brandy, but that's another memoir for another time. If you will indulge me I will get all this shit out of my mind. And we can all get back to having a good time.

THAT'S THE END OF THAT SHIT's!!!

more

pleasantries

on

the

way!!!

After I dried and brushed her hair we returned to the sitting room. The sitting room was the same as the bedroom. There were still lots of munchies available, but it didn't appear as though anyone was in the mood for munchies. And since truth is better than fiction, I shall remind you of both our addictions. I wanted her body and she wanted mine. Her body had a snatch, and I became a snatch smacker. My body had a cock and a bag full of nuts. She was treating my cock like a lollipop and my nuts like hockey pucks. I was finger-slapping her snatch like I was playing the bongos. One nut went left, and one nut went right. Her pussy looked so good I had to take a bite. I covered it up with the palm of my hand, it made a suction cup sound, and she had a grand slam. An orgasmic wonder to centerfield, Babe Ruth or Mickey Mantle would know how that feels.

We played hockey and baseball for the next few hours, with a few timeouts just to smell the flowers, the scent of sex was from wall-to-wall. Loves juices were flowing like Niagara Falls. Sandy rubbed them on her body and I licked them off.

We went from missionary position to a good "ole" 69. Just slipping and sliding with orgasmic rhyme. Our energy was high and nobody lacking, what we brought to life kept us both jacking. When the sun came up, we were still keeping score. I had wracked up 15 more than the night before. Sandy had to be way ahead of me, I can still feel her shaken from number 23. I really liked this gal because we were both the same, just living for love and playing loves game. I never got bothered by her orgasmic goals, I just tried to make them happen by playing my role. She gave so much love in these past two days, and I'd like to repay her in some small way. Then out of nowhere an idea was there, with one forceful thrust of my shaft I declared. "I want you to accompany me, to see the beautiful cherry trees of "ole" DC".

There needs to be something in this love affair, that holds the beauty to compare; with you my lovely lady fair.

So get dressed, or I shall plug your derrière." Damn, that was the wrong thing to say, she tackled me, and I'll never get to see those "ole" cherry trees; But at least that's the end of the poetry.

Her anal opening was so inviting. I knew she had the vegetable oil for something. As she saturated my cock and supervised entry, I was wondering what part the stick of pepperoni was going to play. She must've read my mind. No sooner had that thought came, than she reached for the pepperoni stick. She had a condom to stretch over one end of it. She looked at me and said, "I need a little help, I've never tried this before." I asked, "What do you want me to do? Are you sure you really want to try this?" With a serious look of curiosity on her face, holding and stroking the stick of pepperoni softly she said, "With your cock in my ass, how do I get the pepperoni around to your butt-hole?" I yelled "What!" Sandy very quickly replied, "E-u-u, that was great, your cock just throbbed, and it felt so pronounced inside my ass." Then she smiled and said, "No, seriously, this is for me. But I have never done it before.

I am packed full of you from behind so I'm going to need you to help me spread my pussy for entry." I asked again, "Are you sure you want to do this, it has to hurt." she replied, "Yes, I know it will hurt. But I want to feel the sensation inside of me as it rubs across your cock resting in my ass-hole."

Being concerned and curious I asked, "Where did you get this idea?" She replied, "From the same article I told you about before." Because we possessed pretty much the same characteristics and personality, I tried to exercise sympathy and caution in my response. Then I said, "Okay, it is cherry blossom time. Let's enjoy the scenery and talk a little. If you feel the same when we get back, we'll do it." I gently slipped my cock out of her ass-hole. I kissed her on the cheek while nonchalantly taking the pepperoni stick out of her hand. I laid it up on one of the trays. I then kissed my fingers and softly touched them to her lips. Gently separating her pussy lips, I placed my fingers to the inner lip lining for a short moment and applied light pressure on her clitoris. I completed the final steps of my persuading process by bringing my fingers back to rest in my mouth. Slowly, and sensually, stripping them of all loves-juices with my tongue and lips. I then brought back to her lips, the enjoyment of what remained from the long lasting aromatic flavor by providing a little tender-wet mouth-to-mouth. I said to her, "When we get back, we can read the article together and go from there. But for now, let's take a little time and get a bite to eat." She smiled and said okay. That was the first time I felt I was in control since I met Sandy. It Was like, all of a sudden, she was putty in my hands and was ready to do anything I said.

It was only about a 10 minute walk from Sandy's apartment to the area close to the Washington Monument where the best view of the cherry blossoms could be enjoyed. We spent about an hour just walking around enjoying the view. On our way back we stopped at the White Tower and had a cheeseburger and some fries. Then we headed back to Sandy's apartment to resume our record-setting liaison of illicit lovemaking.

Sandy had already decided to take another sick day. Apparently, she had a number of days built up and had to either use them or lose them. She also took off the next three days, however, she requested them one day at a time. I believe her logic in doing so was to keep me in suspense. Perhaps she felt if she let me know in advance she would be off the rest of the week my enthusiasm to perform might slip to a lackadaisical state. That of course would never happen because of my interest in learning everything she knew or what we could come up with together.

Using each other's bodies and both being mentally and sexually lustful, we were able to create excitement and satisfaction for all of our ideas and desires. With the exception of, the rather large stick of pepperoni. I was able to persuade her to transfer that desire to allowing me to sensually swab her love-nest with hot dogs and Polish sausages. Not only did they provide us with an edible product, but it was quite possibly the safest and certainly least painful of the three. To say nothing of the fact that it helped in keeping our energy level from slipping into the danger zone.

For the remainder of the week we fucked ourselves silly. Sandy was really into keeping track, or should I say, keeping score. She marked down every orgasmic blast that was bestowed upon her. While giving me credit for every little dribble of come I could produce from a busted nut. She maxed out at 27 in one night, and had me down for 19 cosmic-comes. In spite of all the hot dogs and Polish sausages available for consumption I lost 7 pounds that week. We finished out the week on a happy note, a friendly goodbye and, I hope we meet again someday. That would be entirely possible, because I knew exactly where I would be headed for when I decided to leave my hometown.

I got back home on Sunday evening. I had already been scheduled to work on Monday and I knew I would probably see Andrea when she came to pick up whatever groceries she needed. I was extremely anxious to see her and possibly make arrangements to have a meeting so that I could introduce her to some of my new-found sexual pleasures. Unfortunately, I was disappointed when she did not come by to welcome me home. All I could think about was that she might be a little pissed off at me for going away on my vacation. I couldn't go by her house or call her so there was nothing left for me to do wonder. And that's what I did, everything I could possibly think of that could go wrong, in my mind went wrong. Maybe she's decided not to see me anymore. Perhaps she fell back in love with her husband. Or maybe she is just trying to punish me. I guess if she doesn't show up tomorrow, I'll just have to make a dentist appointment so I can talk to her.

As it turned out none of my negative thoughts proved to be true. I guess my old friend, the oddsmaker, was right when he called me a neighboring nabob of negativity. Andrea came by my work the next day. We made arrangements to meet the following day in a nearby town where she did most of her shopping for clothes. Supposedly, her husband would be working. The department store we met at had a snack bar/cafeteria. We

had met there a couple times before. We were having a Coke and talking, I guess it had probably been maybe 10 or 15 minutes. When out-of-the-blue, Andrea said to me in a rather unusual tone, "Brent, please do not question me or look around, just get up and walk straight to the nearest exit right now. I will see you tomorrow or Friday, I hope. Trust me honey, I love you!" Although I had no idea why, I did exactly as she asked. I could tell from the way she made her request, something was seriously wrong.

That evening when I got off from work, I stopped by the gas station to find out everything that happened while I was on vacation. I parked my car and walked over and **sat** down. A couple of the guys got up and walked inside to the back room where they were playing cards. I casually inquired as to what was going on. One of them replied, "I don't know anything, I didn't see anything, and I don't want to hear anything." And he got up walked inside.

The one that remained started laughing, slapped himself on the knee and said, "You are one crazy son-of-a-bitch. I know you're not that brave. It turns out you're not very smart either. You are about to die, and you just walk up here like it ain't no big fuckin' deal." I broke in with, "What the fuck are you talking about man?" He said, "Bullshit, like you didn't know, we all told you what would happen, but you let your prick do your thinking for ya." The man beat the shit out of his wife today and they had to take her to the hospital. Maybe you would like to make another dumb-ass move and go to visit her. Man, he's out here with a gun looking for your ass. So do me a fucking favor, stay the hell away from me. If you survive this, I'll still be your friend, but I never want to know a damn thing you do.

(Favors for dreams in afterglow)
and so said the author

"Becky, you used to call me in the-we-hours of the morning, to make things happen for you. Now I, so many years later, request your return to me in memory. Revive my mind, my heart, and my desire, so that I might relive and bring to life those beautiful memories. Hey baby, you never know, other people might enjoy them just half as much as we did!!!"

CHAPTER 7

The Getaway

T he year was 1962 I was caught in a semi-stable state of sanity between love affairs, politics, and two different types of 38 specials. I have always loved women and found politics interesting. But a gun or firearm of any type has never been a welcome sight to me. Especially, when it is pointed at me with harmful intent on the mind of the pointer. So with not so careful, but expedient consideration, and armed with a letter of reference from my districts State Senator, I found the fastest and safest way out of town.

With no particular place in mind to go, and no particular time to be there, I pulled into a restaurant called the Old Dominion Motel bar and grill. It was a neat little place about 10 miles outside of Washington DC, between Alexandria and Fort Belvoir on route #1. This was an area, which at the time, overwhelmingly supported the nickname "Motel Row".

The restaurant had good home-cooked food. The bar was equipped with live music and dancing, and the motel provided wake up calls. Sort of like a drifters one stop nightly needs. And as it turned out that night, one stop was all I needed.

I sat down at a table in the restaurant and ordered a hamburger with fries and a glass of milk. I must've looked like a stranger because the waitress asked me if this was my first time there. I replied, "Yes ma'am, I'm new in town." She said, "I didn't think I'd seen you here before." As she started to walk away, she continued with, "It's an okay place, you'll probably like it. Oh by the way, my name is Paula and I sing with the band. Our first set starts in about 20 minutes if you're interested." I nodded to her and smiled, she smiled and returned to the kitchen. I finished eating, walked into the bar area, and sat down on a stool at the end of the bar that was closer to the bandstand. I wanted to make sure I could twist around and watch the band. As I turned back to order a beer, I felt somebody tapping me on the shoulder. It was Paula she had my bill from the restaurant in her hand and was waving it with a friendly little smile. I said, "I'm sorry I thought the tab would just carry over." She jokingly informed me that the bar and the restaurant had different managers and they did not trust each other. I gave her a five spot and told her to keep the change. Then I turned around to order a beer. The bartender asked me if I wanted a draft or bottle. I intern asked him, what he had on draft and the prices? He said, "I've got Black label, Gunther, Schaeffer, and old export on draft and everything in the bottle. Draft is $.25 in the bottle is $.30. I opted to have a Black label draft.

The band had been playing maybe 30 minutes and was actually very good. They called themselves the midnighters and sported a rockabilly sort of style, leaning more towards the rock than the billy. With a repertoire of Elvis, Jerry Lee Lewis, Chuck Berry, little Richard, Roy Orbison, Buddy Holly, Connie Francis, Brenda Lee, Johnny Cash, Jack Scott, Web Pierce, Kitty Wells, and a little Hank Williams sr., every now and then. They had obviously been together for quite some time and practiced a lot, as their sound and performance showed. Especially Paula, she was really good. They broke for their first set, so I went in search of the restrooms.

The lighting was very dim for the dance floor area which made it a little difficult to find signs. As I walked back to the bar where I had been sitting, I noticed Paula was in my chair. So I said to her, "Now that you have my seat, could I buy you a drink to hold it for me? I don't want to lose it because you're just too damn good to miss." She replied, "Sure, but let's get a table, I'm off for the next set."

I nodded to the bartender to transfer my tab to the table area. That didn't work either, apparently each area had different managers and they had to keep everything separate. I took care of my bar-tab and followed Paula to her favorite table. It was kind of isolated with two other booths reserved for the band members. After we got seated and ordered the next round of drinks, I asked her, "To what do I owe the pleasure of your company tonight my dear?" She said, "Oh nothing, I was just bored and tired of sitting with the same group of people during the breaks. Besides it's not every day you get to sit with a man in a three-piece suit and patent leather shoes in this bar. Notice how everybody's watching you. They probably think you're recording agent. But I know better." She said with an inquisitive look, and a wink. I asked her, "What do you mean by that?" And she replied, "I think I know who you are. I thought I recognized you in the restaurant, so when I went back into the kitchen I called my sister to see if I was right." I of course immediately inquired, "Who is your sister?" When she told me, from the look on her face, I'm sure she thought I thought I was dead. She grabbed my hand and laughingly said, "It's okay, I'll never tell, this can be our secret as long as you do me one favor." I thought oh my "God", what does she want? Rather hesitantly, I inquired, "After what you know about me what would you possibly be interested in having me do for you?" She consolingly told me, "You're worrying too much, I never liked him anyway. I could never understand what Andrea saw in him. Besides the bands coming back and they're trying out a backup girl singer for me. So I need to listen, and you might enjoy it also. I will let you know what I want later."

We both set kind of quietly listening to the band and the new girl singer. She seemed okay, a little nervous maybe, but I'm sure she would be fine for what they needed her for. The band had started in on Elvis's loving you, so I asked Paula if she would like to dance. The nod was yes and we danced. It was followed by Roy Orbison's, in dreams of you and backed up with Hank Williams's your cheating heart. They kept us in a lover's slow-motion mood for about 10 minutes. Which was all well and good, it gave us an opportunity to do away with small talk and get to know each other better.

CHAPTER 8

The Sexy Sister

Paula was four years older than her sister Andrea. That meant she was six years older than me. I didn't feel too bad because I did not remember Paula, after all, I was in the sixth grade when she was graduating. One thing became increasingly clear, regardless of grades or age we were no longer in school.

Paula, just like her sister, was a very beautiful young lady. Their ancestors very definitely had blessed them with their share of beauty genes. Their mother and father had obviously worked very diligently in putting all the right parts in the right places. I for one would like to have the opportunity to personally congratulate them on the genius of their reproductive expertise. Although I know if I attempted to do so I would probably be shot, since Andrea was the driving force behind her husband's 38 special. It seems a little crazy they all had a special set of 38's. I would certainly rather be confronted with theirs in lieu of his. One of their sets got me in trouble, maybe the other set will get me out of trouble.

All these crazy thoughts are going through my mind while I'm still trying to figure out what favor the second set of 38's is going to ask of me. Of course, there's no mistaking what I would like it to be, but that seems a little far-fetched. Possibly even in the category of a pipedream. But I love to dream, so dream I will.

At the beginning of the second set pause the manager of the band came over to talk to Paula. He told her that she would be doing the next set and he needed to discuss the backup singer with her. Paula stood up and asked me to excuse her and said she would return a little later. She returned to the stage for the beginning of the next set and gave her normal performance of excellence. It seemed to me to include a few little added sexual innuendos for my benefit.

Not soon enough the third set break came. By this time I had consumed a little more happiness beverage than I normally would have. I noticed that Paula, on her way to my table, stopped to talk to her manager. As she walked toward me, she was energetically motioning me to stand up and I did. She said, "They are going to give her a little more stage time, so I'm off for the night. Let's go to another bar so we can talk more freely." Obviously, I had no problem with that. Talking freely with this gorgeous young lady would be something I would enjoy doing.

We went in her car, which unlike most guys, I was quite content with. I always felt if I didn't have to worry about driving my mind was free and so were my hands. We pulled into the parking lot of a country western establishment called the Cowboy Palace. I got out of the car and started walking towards the entrance, suddenly Paula grabbed my arm and we started walking in another direction. In about 100 feet or so we came to a small little building that looked like a double seater outdoor John. If you were any bigger than a popcorn-fart, you wouldn't fit inside. Paula already had a key. She unlocked the door and pulled me inside, then shut and locked the door behind us.

Given the history of our family relationships I was a little unnerved, so I said, "What the hell you doing?" With no response she grabbed and favored me with a lip lock that would make the jaws of life seem like a pair of pliers. I exclaimed "Wait, I need more room to operate." I had no sooner said that than she pulled off my coat pushed me up against the wall and said, "Honey, if you need any more room than this then you don't need me. I am a fast-fuck and I know how to turn a buck, but this one for you is free. Oh, by the way, what is your first name? I never give freebies without first names."

I told her my name and she said, "That's a nice name. Wow Brent, I feel like I have known you forever. I hope you are as good as Andrea said because I am totally primed, so lets get this show on the road."

In a heartbeat our clothes were off. We were rolling around on what was supposed to be a floor, and bouncing off the walls. This place was great, you couldn't hurt yourself if you tried. It was like a padded cell. Everything was soft except my cock and her nipples. Paula's nipples were to the touch like that of an uncommonly soft rigid velvet texture, with a deep dark circular overlay that bubbled about the outer rim while pronouncing perfection personified and begging to be orally pleasured. She had nipples that demanded an orgasmic response for the sheer pleasure of viewing. **Excuse me, emergency delivery!!!** And so it comes, and so it comes, and so it comes, now they are covered with come. Youthfulness is wonderful, I had plenty to spare. Paula was enjoying her bath. She was massaging her upper torso, tits and face with my come, and streaming her fingers through her hair.

We were rolling around on top then bottom no longer bouncing, we were sliding from wall-to-wall of the whole 48 square feet in that little 6 x 8 sex shack. It was equipped with a fold down cott that we had absolutely no use for. And you know what, we hadn't even got to the *down and dirty read'em and weep nitty-gritty* yet.

Suddenly, Andrea crossed my mind, what happened to her? Did this first set of 38's get all the nympho-characteristics? To be continued, it's getting late and I'm tired. I shall have to wait until tomorrow to see what happens next, or at least, till after my next dream.

I woke up the next morning 10 minutes before checkout time, which was 11 AM. Not having anything pressing that I was supposed to do, I just thought screw this, called the front desk re-upped for another day and went back to sleep.

It was about 2 PM when I finally got out of bed. I called the front desk for room service and a pot of coffee. The operator kind of chuckled and said, "I don't know where you think you are Rockefeller, but this ain't the Hilton. There's a 7- Eleven across the street, that's the nearest thing to room service I got for you."

I looked through my suitcase for something to wear, went across the street picked up two large cups of coffee and a pack of cigarettes. Then I headed back to my room.

That in itself, turned out to be quite interesting. I found out very quickly traffic in this area was nuts, nobody waits for nobody.

After almost being ran over twice, some overly friendly driver with an IQ gesture yelled, "Get to fuck the crosswalk and wait for the traffic light hayseed." It sounded like good advice and the sensible thing to do since everybody else was, so that's what I did. I got back to my motel started up to my room when the desk clerk stopped me and informed me that I must pay the next days rent before they would let me in.

It seemed like they didn't trust me and had put a key plug in my lock. I paid my bill and he accompanied me to my room to remove the plug from my door lock. By this time I was totally awake, and sober. The coffee wasn't necessary but I drank it anyway, and tried to understand the difference from my hometown to here.

I took a shower then dressed and was on my way to explore the attractions of the city. I was in no hurry to use my letter of reference, or even think about getting a job, especially after last night. I was still kind of in a shock from all that, but not so much so that I wasn't going to go back and try to do it all over again tonight.

I kept wondering what the favor she wanted from me was. After all the favors she bestowed upon me last night I was not going to spend too much time worrying about it, I had other things to do.

Like get a little familiar with the area and take in some of the sights, what could I possibly do to equal that. Taking in the sights was the best part. It led me to the monument and the reflection pool area with the paddle boats.

I knew right away I was going to like this area. While walking through the monument grounds to the reflection pool I was greeted by what seemed to be a ratio of maybe 5 to 1. With young ladies occupying the five, and that was no problem at all for me to accept.

In a matter of 15 minutes, I had been invited to lunch at three different on the ground picnic settings. I guess for the right guy it seemed like an all you can eat buffet, ranging from fried chicken to chocolate chip cookies. prepared by fine looking young ladies serving white wine as the favorite beverage.

I partook of a bite here and there, got a phone number or two, explaining my situation and that I had no phone number to give them at this time. All in all it was a very productive and enjoyable afternoon. I gave it considerable thought on my way back to my room.

I took my suit off and laid down across the bed to rest a few minutes before getting ready for the evenings anticipated events. I was quite curious and extremely anxious to find out what Paula had in mind for this evening.

I got up showered, shaved, and dressed then went down to the bar. Only to find out that Paula was no longer a member of the Midnighter's, and that I should leave without asking questions. I guess something involving me didn't set right with the band leader. So I left, but on my way out I stopped at the restaurant and found out that Paula still worked there and she would be on the afternoon shift the next day.

Well now I was screwed, blued, and almost tattooed, as that old saying goes. I had really been looking forward to seeing and being with Paula again this evening. I decided to check out a few places on the strip and maybe find a little action that would meet my satisfaction.

As I'm driving I started thinking, well maybe I'll go to the Cowboy Palace and see what's going on there. Since we started to go there last night it was almost like a magnet. As I pulled into the entrance, off to the right I could see the little 6 x 8 sex shack and a déjà vuic orgasmic memory flooded my mind. I almost busted a nut just thinking about it.

I reclaimed my thoughts and walked in the front door, which led to the bar and the dance hall. It was too early to eat so I got a beer, besides they had small bowls of complimentary pretzels and popcorn all along the bar. There weren't many people at the bar, so I struck up a conversation with the bartender. During the next five minutes he gave me his life story and the history of the Cowboy Palace. He also explained the reason for all the little 6 x 8' motels, as he called them. I guess it makes sense, two military bases within 25 miles of each other on the same road. The soldiers all go barhopping on the weekend trying to pick up girls. Most of the time they have too much to drink and cannot drive back to their base. They need a place to have sex or a little sleep.

Apparently, the main highway was lined with these little 6 x 8' money making sleeper shacks. Hence the nickname, Motel Row. Personally, after my experience from last night, I prefer to think of them as sex shacks and believe he was feeding me a line of crap as a cover up. I can't imagine sleeping quarters that small, especially if they got lucky and had a friend.

He also told me the Cowboy Palace was the best fast track country music place in the area. Every night they have three different bands that play three 40 minute sets apiece. There are no breaks, they change between songs from 8 PM until 2 AM, and we have a $5.00 cover charge. He had obviously spent a lot of time memorizing his spiel. It was more than I needed to know. I could have done fine with, if you are still here at 8 PM, $5.00 will be added to your bar tab.

I checked my watch it was 6:15, two hours before the action starts. I ordered another draft and sat there thinking about what I should do. When I finished my beer I paid the tab walked outside and headed toward my car. As I started to open the door I looked up and saw Paula pulling into the parking lot. She got out of her car and started walking in the direction of that same little sex shack we went to last night.

How did she know I was here? I could feel that certain tingling sensation starting to enter my loin area. Suddenly I was on fire for her, and as I began to walk around my car I said, "Paula, wait for me I'm coming." Which was damn near the truth. She turned and saw me then said with a considerable amount of shock and surprise in her voice. "Brent, what the hell are you doing here? Come back to the bar later, I'll see you there." As she continued on Her Way, Paula started moving her arms and muttering to herself. She stopped to unlock the door and was almost shouting, "fuck, fu-ck, fuck me!" That was exactly what I had in mind, except she looked and sounded pissed-off and frustrated.

Oh well, so was I, maybe I can find a block of ice to sit on until I can regain my composure.

If I were back home, I could find somebody to handle my problem. I must make sure this will be the last time I get a homesick for a cock pleaser. There are lots of paddle boat baby's and picnic cuties around, surely, I can find a steady standby to console me in my time of need.

I was about to go back into the bar for another drink when out of nowhere this strange feeling hit me like a ton of bricks. It was a, you need to take a break feeling. So instead, I got in my car and drove back to my motel.

I went up to my room and fell on my bed clothes and all. I remember thinking just before I fell asleep, damn this is a fast-moving place, I am not used to this. If I am going to survive here I will have to adjust my mind to fit the pace.

When I woke up it was almost 9 o'clock. I took a quick shower and dressed but decided not to go to the Cowboy Palace. I had probably already missed Paula anyway, so I thought I might head over the bridge towards Maryland. One of my friends back home had some relatives that lived in Waldorf. From what they told him the nightlife there never ended. The slot machines, or, one-armed bandits, were on fire. There was big name entertainment all the time. It sounded good to me. Now all I had to do was find Waldorf.

CHAPTER 9

My Slot Machine Lover

I had been driving for a while, I guess maybe 40 or 45 minutes before I saw Waldorf city limit sign. Man, what a place, I drove up one side and down the other. It must have been a mile or a mile and a half stretch. Both sides were full, something there for everybody. I pulled into what looked like might be one of the larger establishments called the Wigwam.

The marquis said Ronnie Dove, one night only. The place was packed, so I squeezed my way through the crowd up to the bar to get a drink. There was no place to sit so I worked my way back to the little alleys where the slot machines were. I knew absolutely nothing about slot machines and wanted to know less, but I had noticed on the way in that's where the ladies were.

As I casually strolled through the one-armed-bandit area it became very obvious the excitement and thrills, especially the ladies, were receiving from dropping money into that little machine. While simultaneously grabbing a handle that was shaped similar to a penis and pulling on it. If they were lucky enough to win, they would treat it as though it were an orgasm. Some of them were screaming and waving their arms around while jumping up and down.

Sometimes they would take the coins they won and rub them all over the nape of their neck and on the upper part of their breasts, allowing them to slip down into their bra. I figured it must be a logical explanation for this type of response, so I didn't question it. I did, however, make a quick decision determining this would be where I would spend my time.

I had already made a comparison calculation which resulted in about a 10 to 1 ratio in favor of ladies. I knew with the odds in my favor that much, I would have a very good chance of adding some unexpected excitement to at least one of the lady handle pullers evening.

It was at that very moment I had a memory of a conversation between myself, my uncle Gene, and my father. We had been sitting around shooting the crap about different things, when Uncle Gene suddenly broke in with a story about women being slot machines and handle pulling lovers. He apparently had been around a few areas in his travels that allowed slot machines as one of their forms of entertainment and revenue.

The one thing I remember of his added attraction comments to the conversation was, "You've got to watch the body language. If you see a lady that is physically caressing, molesting, or seducing the machine, that is a tell-tale sign. It begins with her facial expressions. If her mouth opens slightly and her jaw jack's a little sideways while her tongue feverishly caresses the upper lip more so than the lower. When her knees start moving in unison and her hips are swaying between the mamba and the twist as she inserts her coins, she's ready. The slightest touch of your hand to hers as she pulls the penis shape handle will make you both the recipient of a climatic interlude and she will be going home with you. Mainly because she's not getting enough attention at her own home. It may be sad but it's probably true. And at that point it is your responsibility to erase her sadness and increase her pleasure. Nothing is more painful than to see a lovely lady laden with loneliness. I mean, it pulls and drags at your loins until it dictates your comings and goings. All you need is to remember that you were born to please." I always liked my Uncle Gene. He had a certain way of getting right to the point. His point had been made and met by a young lady I had noticed earlier and was now the center-point of my attention.

She had long wavy, shiny black hair, and was feeding coins to the slot machine like there was no tomorrow. She had no room for sadness and no room for sorrow. One hand feeding the other one pulling, she was loving that machine. I reached up and touched her hand just as a bell started ringing. Coins were falling everywhere. She turned and grabbed me then started jumping up and down and screaming 777 I think I'm in heaven. We danced and bounced together around and around for what seemed like forever. She looked at me and said, "Let's gather up this shit and go somewhere."

I don't know how much money she won. I do know that it was enough to pay for the best room in the room at the Wigwam Motel. Her name was Becky, her favorite wine was Manischewitz, and mine was whatever turned her on.

That night I felt like I had lived up to my expectations according to Uncle Gene. From the touch of my hand her sadness was turned to happiness. I thought Uncle Gene was a genius or some sort of a mastermind on the art of slot machine lovers.

We had one hell of a good time and what turned into a super good night. Unbelievable things happened on that king size bed. Things I never thought would or could happen in my life. We were slipping and sliding trying to find what we were hiding. We put things in places I know were lost forever. And that lady became my lady love and long lifetime friend.

She taught me so much more than I knew before, and I knew we would be friends forever. Becky loved the slot machines, and I loved her machine. It brought to mind an old country cliché, probably written by some hungry trucker for a waitress at a truck stop. **"Ham and eggs between your legs pork chops and gravy,**

your machine and my machine will drive us both crazy." Becky turned out to be my lifelong soul mate. And I was the same for her. She knew what I wanted and needed. I knew what she wanted and needed. Though we were not together our minds and our hearts were as one. If she had a problem, she knew I had a plan. If I had a problem, I knew she had a plan. All we ever had to do was make a phone call and all the problems were solved. The crazy thing to know is that our lives were brought together by one unbelievable slot machine love night. Hell, it was still like that when I retired. I bet if I had a problem today all I would have to do be make a phone call, and the same would be for her.

Life could not have been better, the hell with a job or a reference letter. I had found my true calling, and was born for balling. I said, "Baby I love women that like to get funky, so lay down here and start slapping my monkey. Now smile a while and give your face a rest, while I erupt in volcanic fashion all across your breasts. Spread it from nipples to tongue with your fingers and lace and let me bring you pleasure as you sit on my face.

When she stood up her slot machine began dropping coins. I quickly grabbed her arm and started cranking as though she were one arm bandit. She followed by coordinating her coin drops with my arm cranks. Becky had perfect pussy muscle control. It was like she had done this many times before, or been practicing, maybe she had.

We got another glass of wine and some more Vaseline and went back to bed to see who could make the largest coin deposit. Becky loved playing sex games and so did I but she always won. Her windows were open 24 hours a day. I have made love to her so many times while she was asleep. I'd tell her about next day and she'd say she knew but she just thought she was dreaming. Same thing would go for me. I used to wake up and she would be topside. I would yawn and bite her on the nipple and asked if she was enjoying her ride. No more time for sleepy sex. Now it's time to sleep and live to play another day. **More to Kum!!!**

I was awakened many times throughout the night and morning, without warning of her lips around my cock and balls. It was quite obvious Becky had her shit together. And knew just how she wanted the game to play out. I became aware of that when I was brought to consciousness by the overwhelmingly sexual body overtones of my entire nut sack and cock in her mouth, while double-finger-fucking me in the ass-hole with a Vaseline covered rubber stretched over her fingers. There was no need or desire for sleep. This woman knew what love making was all about, she was fantastically unbelievable. Becky could create an orgasmic response by taking a piece of ice from your wine glass, sensually caressing it with her lips and sticking it ever so teasingly, where the sun don't shine. In other words. Up your ass!!! Becky was not only a good lover she was a great loving machine.

She didn't need to eat, she didn't need to sleep. She got her energy and nutrition from fucking, sucking, and swallowing kum, while penetrating your anus with her thumb. I knew she was the one I wanted to learn from, and she made it obvious she enjoyed teaching me. That just made everything "hunky-dory." All we had to do was fuck and suck, eat and sleep, except Becky didn't need sleep. My sleep was constantly interrupted by the different ways and places she chose for vegetable oil saturation. We gave a whole new meaning to slipping and sliding, bumping and grinding, filling every crack and crevice, armpit, ear and nostril with an overdose of loves lotion. I loved to titty-fuck Becky because I could get off twice as much by just thinking about or watching her as she stretched her tongue to the tip of her nose to lick the extra juices as they ran down over her face and cheeks. Becky had the perfect size tits for titty-fucking. She could always tell by the feel of my cock between her tits when it was time to lower her chin slightly and opened her mouth so I could allow the "ole" Jizzum Trail to open its flood gates and give her tonsils a kum-shower. She would start moving, moaning, and go crazy. She made it seem like she had never had anything to eat or to drink. Or at least nothing that taste that good. Becky was something special and filled with bedtime pleasures. She was a crazy, crazy love-maker that knew no boundary's, with no holds barred. Her animalistic characteristics surfaced in the bedroom and she turned you into an animal as well. she was able to turn the tables in a way that you became her and she became you. Becky was the perfect person I needed to teach me everything I wanted to know and maybe even a little bit more.

I must have either passed-out or fell asleep while Becky was sucking my cock. The last thing I remember was her trying to swallow my entire body while her nostrils were breathing fire up my ass-hole. I woke up and had to go to the bathroom. I was holding my head to make sure it was still there. As I returned I noticed the clock said 4, and I thought, oh shipped, I am fucked. Checkout time at my Motel in Virginia was 11 AM. I was 40 or 50 miles away and it was 4 PM.

I started looking around for a phone, in the process I found my clothes and started dressing. When suddenly I got attacked from behind and was pulled down on to the bed. I was improperly placed spread-eagle half-dressed looking up at a sex-crazed woman that had only one thing on her mind. That was to spend all the money she had won and have fun doing it while leaving all her worries behind.

I was so fucking tired, but glad she picked me to help her accomplish her goals. It was very plain that she liked playing boss from that top-side dominating position. Becky could be my **"Boss Lady"** anytime. Her wish was my command, except when I remembered my suitcase and clothes were at my Motel.

I proceeded to try to inform Becky that I must pay my Motel bill and get my clothes. I can't even imagine what my request sounded like because she was so busy feeding me left nipple right nipple, no favoritism could be shown. Over and over again while her other hand was force-feeding my cock from her pussy to her ass-hole, and back and forth, and back and forth.

As I think back, once again I must give thanks to my youth. I must've had five, ten, or maybe fifteen orgasms. I didn't even try to count, I just kept coming. Then suddenly the bed started shaking, the lights seemed to be flickering, or else I was blinking my eyes really fast. Becky's entire body started to quiver as though an earthquake was taking place inside her. Then with a pain-filled pleasurable scream she collapsed and flooded me and the bed.

I thought to myself, how great was that? Damn, I have never seen anything like that before. But it was a fun game to be a part of, even if I was an amateur player. I had the feeling I would not be holding amateur status long if I hung out with her for a while. I whispered to myself, "Thank you Becky, I will do better the next time!!!"

The next time was only a matter of moments. Becky got up and totally uninhibited, without saying a word, started walking towards the bathroom. With each step she took Becky was purposely swaying that naked-larger-than-life hour-glass-shaped body with sexual intent for my eyes only. She was twirling, and rolling, her long sexy jet black hair into a bun on the top of her head.

So many little turn-on moves in that process. I felt like tackling her and fucking the hole in the perfectly prepared bun she had properly placed so my balls would bounce around on her forehead if I tried. She even made the bun look sexy. I wondered if she could have an orgasm from that. I bet she could. Maybe I'll try that sometime. Man, she was good, and knew exactly what she was doing to me. Becky was built for speed with a-lot-a-need. If I live through her pleasures I will be ready for anything.

I heard the shower stop running. Then I saw this voluptuously desirable water dripping piece of female flesh, seducing me softly with every move she made. Her long dark hair was jolting from side-to-side behind her, as her body produced an even more special cat-walk kind of seductive strut while approaching the bed.

She had two large towels. One she spread out on the bed to lay down on. The other one she handed to me and began to instruct me on how pat her body dry.

I had nearly finished when I noticed a trickle of water making its way from her bellybutton to the connecting valley of her hip and enter-thigh, in route to her recently padded dry love nest. I suddenly had the urge not to use the towel. So I lowered my face to her area of wetness and teasingly tongued while lip-sucking the escaping water away. I immediately felt Becky's hand on my head. She began moving my head slowly to position my tongue in the area that guarded her prize possession. The earthquake maker, her clitoris, I gently touched my tongue to her clit and started softly rolling it around with a slow circular motion when suddenly Becky grabbed my hair lifted my head and said, "Hold that thought."

Then in what seemed like one body bounce off the bed, she landed up-right on her feet. Put on a pair of shorts, sandals, and what looked like an old crunched up fishing hat, and said, "Be back in a bit." I didn't question, as a matter-of-fact, I thought I could use the time to take a shower, brush my teeth, and maybe catch a nap.

I had just got out of the shower and was standing in front of the mirror drying my hair when I heard the door open. It had only been 10 or maybe 15 minutes since Becky left, that can't be her, I thought as I yelled, "Is that you Becky?" I was answered by an unfamiliar voice, "No it's Sandy, Becky gave me her key and said to tell you she would be here in a minute. Until then, you are Brent and I'm Sandy, so let's have a drink and get to know each other while we wait." I wasn't sure what to think but it sounded okay so I replied, "That sounds good to me, the ice is in the fridge and there is Southern Comfort and Manichewitz on the counter. You fix them and I'll get dressed, oh yeah, there is beer in the fridge if you don't want the other." She quickly responded, "Oh no, I don't know how to mix drinks, just come on out, it's ok."

I didn't have any idea who she was, but I had learned that things happened differently and much faster in this area than I was accustomed to. I wrapped a towel around my waist and went out to meet Sandy. Then I acted like I was a professional bartender and fixed our drinks. She nodded yes to the Southern Comfort, so I made us both a double.

I didn't know where this was going but I figured two or three doubles would help unlock the doors and get us there quicker. I could feel the towel begin to loosen at my waist so I turned a little to one side and secured it.

As I turned back, Sandy asked with a question-mark smile, "So where did you meet Becky?" I replied, "Well, I was hanging out in the slot machine rows when I spotted a young lady that appeared to be sexually harassing the one- armed-bandit she was feeding. I thought maybe she needed a little tender touch to calm her down. I walked over to where she was, and just as I reached up to help her pull down the stick, bells started ringing and money was falling everywhere. Becky started screaming and jumping up and down, she thought she was in heaven. She had hit the jackpot on 777 and needed someone to help her spend it and make all her troubles go away. I guess she thought I was her lucky charm, so she picked me."

About that time, I heard, "And that is exactly how it happened." It was Becky, Sandy must have left the door unlocked for her because I didn't hear her come in. Then she started telling Sandy all about it again, so I started to walk into the other room to get dressed. Becky reached out and grabbed me. She looked down at my towel and put her hand inside the twisted part. Then with the lust-filled lure of a lady wanting more than she was asking for, said to me as she put the tender-touch of a ball-roll on my nut-sack, "Might I have a little drink before you go, bartender?" I said, "Ye-s ma'am," as I joined in on her hand-grinding process, "You sure can." I fixed her a drink while they talked about her winnings and my towel. I handed the drink to her and bowed, as I exited the room, Becky pulled my towel away.

I got totally dressed except for my jacket, and I was carrying it. As I entered the living room area from the bedroom, I noticed Becky and Sandy were kissing. I thought, wow, how cool is this, what's up next? About that time Becky realized I was coming into the room. She moved a little to one side and said, "I called your motel manager while I was out. I know him pretty well, he's a friend of mine. Everything there is okay, so why don't you go on back to Virginia and take care of what you need to. I will catch up with you a little later. Sandy and I need a little time together to straighten a few things out." I said, "Okay, I can do that. I do need to take care of some business there." I walked over to Becky and gave her a kiss on the cheek and said, "You are an unbelievably super lady, I'll see you later." I said goodbye to Sandy and left.

When I got to the elevator two men started to get off. I guess they realized it was the wrong floor and got back on. I never thought anything about it at the time. I got on the elevator and pressed the first-floor button, went to the parking lot, got in my car and headed to Virginia.

While I was driving, I could not help thinking, what a great place this was and how glad I was that I decided to come here. Everyone seems so nice and friendly, and it seemed like all the women wanted what I wanted, which of course, was a steady diet of lovemaking.

Meanwhile, when I arrived at the motel I found out my room rent had been paid for a week. I thought to myself, man, I gotta do something great for that lady. But there was one thing for certain, before I could do anything great or otherwise, I needed to get some sleep, and sleep I did.

When I woke up it was dark, I didn't wear a watch, the only one I had was a pocket watch and for my vest. I turned on the light to see if the radio had a clock. It did not, so I found my pocket watch and saw it was almost 9:30pm. I shaved, brushed my teeth and took a shower.

While I was getting dressed I got ambushed by hunger pains. My body was in bad need of a steak, or carbohydrates of some sort. I remembered that while I had been driving on route #1 a couple nights before, I passed an Italian restaurant called Mama Mia's.

I love Italian food. I also like the stories about the Mafia and how when they all went to eat the boss always sat with his back to the wall. And when he ordered his meal, he ordered a shot glass of olive oil with it. And so it was, with my back to the wall an order of spaghetti and meatballs with a shot glass of olive oil, that night, I was the boss. I took my time and enjoyed the meal and the atmosphere, which was very mob-like. In a few minutes a different waitress brought my check. I wasn't paying much attention because I was enjoying Mama's meatballs and picturing myself as a mob-boss with an entourage of sergeants in a restaurant in Sicily.

Suddenly I heard, "Fancy meeting you here, I thought I'd never see you again." I awakened from my trance only to see one of the gorgeous young ladies I had the pleasure of meeting while she was paddling her boat by the Jefferson Memorial. Her name tag said Roxanne, so I didn't quibble with that, I just said, "Hi Roxanne, how are you doing? What are you doing here?" I think she thought I didn't recognize her, so she responded with, "I only get to pack lunches, and paddleboats, on the weekends. I have to work sometimes, and I work here."

I tried to play it off like I thought she worked for the park authority, and that paddling the paddle boats was part of her job to provide scenery and entertainment for tourists. But she informed me that was her form of weekend entertainment, when she could afford it.

Roxanne was one of the paddle boat girls that I had met a few days before. Unfortunately, she must not have made much of an impression on me. I had neglected to get her phone number. Which I now realized, was an oversight on my behalf.

She, like the other paddle boat baby's, had a very good figure, along with an abundant amount of desire in her smile and body language. She also had the most beautiful shade of red hair I think I'd ever seen. Her long wavy red hair was filling my mind with fantasies of how body parts could get lost there.

When I finally realized I was in a restaurant and had to pay my bill, I looked up and she was staring at me. Then she said, "Like, where are you?" I told her the truth, that I was having a dream about her beautiful red hair. Then I took the check, and asked, "Do you work here every night during the week?" She replied, "Yes, and every other weekend." And I said, "Damn why do you work so much?" Then she told me this was her second job and she also went to school two nights a week at Northern Virginia community college.

The first thing on my mind was, this girl is too busy, to get busy. I put 10 bucks on the check and said, "Hopefully I'll see you again, I like Italian food." As she was picking up the money and the check, she very nonchalantly, wrote her phone number down on the corner of the place mat. Then, in a rather friendly, maybe even inviting way she said, "I'll be here." As I was leaving, I tore the corner of the place mat with the phone number on it off and walked out.

As I was walking to my car I started thinking, she's a redhead. I had always been told that redheads were hot, but they also had bad tempers. That was something I didn't feel I needed any part of. I do not like the idea of a girl being mad, or, pissed off. Too many bad things can happen. I dropped her number in the ashtray and never thought any more about it at the time.

When I pulled back out on the highway I suddenly became. Engulfed in a rather large group of cars. They were all filled with high school kids hanging out the windows and waving their arms in a manner that might lead you to believe they had just won a ballgame and was going someplace to celebrate a victory. I thought, that was always a fun thing to do. I followed them to see where the celebration would take place.

It came to an abrupt halt with police officers stopping all traffic, so they could safely make a left-hand turn across the highway. That led them into a parking lot of what appeared to be a one-story long barn-like looking building. At first I thought it was a carwash but it turned out to be a teenage-juke joint, or, hang-out.

I was about to try to exit the parking lot and leave when I saw another one of my paddle-boat-baby's. She was the driver of one of the cars, which I found out later was accompanied by her younger sister and a couple friends. I guess that meant she was the chaperone. This was one that had made an impression on me at the time and I was able to get her name and phone number. It took me a second, but I remembered her name, it was Marlene. I guess the group of paddle boat baby's must have lived in the same area. I was a couple cars away from her when they directed us into parking spaces so I thought I would see if she remembered me. I got out and stood beside my car, when she opened her door to get out, I said, "Marlene." She looked as though she did not recognize me, so I had to think of something quick. Since it was Friday night and the weekend was close, I said, "I know I'll be hungry tomorrow, are you going paddle boating again?" She replied, with a questioning look, "No, we can't all get together this weekend." It did not seem like she wanted to continue the conversation, but I had to keep it going because I wanted to get to know her better, and I said, "I just ran into Roxanne, you know her don't you?" She nodded her head indicating yes then said, "I really have to get inside with my sister, maybe I'll see you another time when you're checking out the paddle boat picnic scene."

I watched as she was walking away to see if maybe she would give me a glance back, but no such luck. I thought, wow, we got along pretty good when I met her. After all she gave me her name and phone number. Oh well, you can't win them all. But I sure can try, and I headed back out onto route #1.

My mind was kind of in limbo as far as knowing where I was headed. It had to be 10:30, maybe even 11 o'clock. So, I thought I would just drive around aimlessly to see what, or who, I could get into.

CHAPTER 10

My Cherie

About a half-hour later, after making several turns onto unknown roads, I ended up in an interesting little place called the Dolphin Restaurant. I had noticed as I was waiting to be seated, the waitresses were very scantily clad in see-through attire. One in particular, in high heeled shoes and a transparent négligée, with nothing on under it. She was dancing on three tables that seemed to have been pulled together to accommodate a large party. They were all very easy on the eyes, and heavy on the mind. Which I am sure could be blamed on the proprietor.

The hostess walked up to me and ask if I was alone. I told her I was but had just eaten. However, my mind's-eye had suddenly developed an entirely different kind of hunger. She smiled and motioned for me to follow her. She made her way through the rather crowded tables to a smaller single seat booth and said, "How's this?" I told her it was fine and thanked her. As she laid the menu down, she said, "We have no cover charge, but there is a three-drink minimum." I said, "That's fine, I'll have a Black label." She immediately reiterated, "There is a three-drink minimum, but a five-beer minimum. I just naturally thought by the way you were dressed you would be having mixed drinks instead of beer, I'm sorry." I assured her it was okay, and she need not apologize. Then she said, "The first five are payable in advance, you may pay one at a time after that." I let her know I understood and started thinking, they not only want your money, but they want you to get screwed up too. As though the dancers were not enough to achieve that objective. In a minute or two a lovely young waitress with almost nothing on was approaching my table with a sensually-sexy-strut. Her next to nothing attire was accompanied by a sultry smile that said, **come and get me, I dare you.**

Then she put a small bucket of ice with five beers in it along with a check on the table and said, "That will be $15 please. My name is Chérie, and if you need some company, I am yours." I thought to myself, this place is pretty cool, and slid over a little in the booth to make room for her to sit down and said, "Why thank you very much. I would love to have the pleasure of your company Chérie." I partially stood up and made a hand gesture to the seat I had cleared for her and said, "Please, why don't you just place that nearly uncovered gorgeous treasure of yours on this little section of seat and order yourself a drink, or have a beer?"

And sit down she did, I had never been the recipient of a sit-down performance like the one she gave. I think everyone in that bar applauded her twirl around upside down, turn around, double backflip perfect landing with a smile and a bow, while all the time looking at me.

Now I knew, I was all that, in high school. And girls were just waiting for me to make a move. That was high school, and this was an erotic sex bar, for which I really had no answer. Except for the possibility that maybe the requirements to become a waitress here are that you have taken gymnastics and erotic dancing classes. I put 10 bucks on the table and gave her a standing ovation with applause along with everybody else awaiting the encore performance. And so it came, what a magnificent specimen of female flesh Chérie portrayed across her table-clothed arena. She never touched the floor with her bare feet. She came to rest with her back, thrust flat on my table with one knee up in the air and the other being pressed down and serving as a footrest. She leaned forward slightly on one elbow and looked at me with a smile. The applause was unbelievable, I didn't know if she was a cheerleader or an Olympic dancer. In my mind, Chérie could have been whatever the hell she wanted to be at that time. Her performance was absolutely perfect and so was she.

I felt compelled to dig deeper into my wallet and I did just that. I honestly don't know how deep, I wasn't looking or counting. All I knew was she sure as hell impressed me and I was looking to harness some of her energy if I possibly could. And I guess the rest is history, though somewhat of a mystery.

As I thought back, I was really glad that my aunt and uncle had set up a trust fund for me. If not for that I would never have been able to be enjoying the pleasures of life that I was now being subjected to.

I woke up the next morning in an uncomfortable position, at the same table, in the same bar that I last remember from the night before. I guess I spent enough money they felt it would be okay if I slept it off.

I slowly made my way to daylight holding my hand above my eyes to shade the light. I looked around to where I thought I had parked my car but couldn't find it. I reached into my pocket to get my keys but there were no keys. I thought, what the hell is this, where is my car?

I could barely see, either the sun was so bright, or my eyes were so bad. I really needed my sunglasses. Of course, they would naturally be in my car. Still shading my eyes, I started scanning the area and spotted a Little Tavern restaurant. I knew they had coffee and hamburgers, so I headed that way.

The guy working behind the counter took my order and asked me if I had been at the Dolphin last night. I told him I had and that

I seem to have misplaced my car and my keys somewhere. Then he asked, "Do you drive a red and white 57 Chevy hard-top with a continental kit?" I looked up at him inquiringly and said, "That's right!" He opened his cash register, picked up some keys and said, "You must have been a damn good customer. They've never done this before, that I know about."

He laid my keys down in front of me and smiled. He said, "Chérie brought your car and keys over about 5 AM, she's my sister, I'm Ronnie." We shook hands and I said, thanks man, that's great, and you have a really nice sister." He said, "Yeah, you like her?" I replied, yeah man she's cool, oh by the way, is my car okay?" He told me yes it was fine and how nice he thought it looked. They had parked it out back where he could see it from the kitchen. We talked for a couple minutes, then he finally said, "Well, I hope you have enough money left to pay your check." I inquired, "What makes you say that? He replied, "Oh nothing, it just sounded like you were having a good time. And that usually means you spent a lot of money."

I nodded yes, got up and went to the bathroom. I did so mainly to check my wallet since I my head wasn't letting my memory work. I splashed some cold water on my face which helped a little, oops, no money. Fortunately for me this was in the days that money belts had become popular. Uncle Gene had bought me one as a going away present. He also told me, don't just wear it, put something in it. You never know what you're gonna need, especially in the area you are headed for.

I took out a 20 and stuck it in my shirt pocket and slapped a little more, cold water on my face. Then I went out and paid my check. I told Ronnie to tell his sister I said thanks very much. He said he would and handed me my change. I told him not to worry about it, that was for looking after my car and keys. I went out back and looked around and my car just to satisfy myself. I opened the door and sat down, got my sunglasses and thanked "God" for being so good to me and keeping me safe and out of trouble. I Put my car in reverse and turned around to look out the back window, on the backseat was a rather large cardboard poster that said. "Brent, thanks for everything, come back and see me, or call. She left her phone number, and it was signed, Cherie.

I thought that was pretty nice of her, I guess I spent enough money to satisfy someone other than myself. I wasn't exactly sure what I wanted to do today it was still a little too early to think straight, so I headed back to my room. That took a little more time because I had no idea where I was in relation to my motel.

I got back to my room about 12 o'clock and decided I would take a quick shower and try to catch a nap. I was awakened by a very light tapping on my door. It was a wonder it woke me, but it did.

I put my pants on as I was walking to the door wondering who it could be. When I opened the door, I was zipping up my fly and my head was kind of bowed a little. Then I heard a frighteningly familiar female voice say, "Don't put it away, I was hoping it would be available for play." As I looked up, I said, "Hel-lo." It was Paula's beautiful married sister, Andrea. I could only dream about what I hoped she was there for.

I inquired, "Are you trying to get me shot? You know I left town so I would not get shot. But my dear, it is so good to see you I shall take my chances." I stepped back a little bit, bowed slightly and said, **"Bring that gorgeously sexy hunk of female flesh to me!!!** My bed is still warm. Hell, it might even be wet. I was right in the middle of one of my favorite moves when you visit me in my dreams."

She smiled, laughed slightly, then reached for my crotch and said, "You lie, you're not even ready. But give me a second and I'll fix that." That was our normal way of talking to each other. Every move, every word was full of innuendos with sexual overtones that related to the down and dirty read-em and weep, nitty-gritty bouncing moves of pussy and prick with the occasional popping of the prune. Which involved the fucking and sucking of every or opening possible to penetrate or suckle. Armpits and titty-fucking always fulfilled my favorite flavor desires with Andrea. The nape of the knee was for some reason very appealing to me, especially her knee. Andrea was just too sexy for words. I could fuck her bellybutton and get off while sucking her toe. And she felt the same way about me.

Our relationship involved nothing but sex. And that's all we needed, when we would meet, we would never go out to eat. We ate each other, and the nourishment was overwhelming. Nothing was off-limits or out of bounds for us. Andrea could have an orgasm while sucking my fingers, my toes, my earlobe's, my nose, or licking my ass. I in turn could bust a nut while visiting the same unorthodox areas. When we finally decided to give the bed a break and get a drink of water to prevent dehydration brought about by the overindulgence of bodily pleasures, or, orifice explosions, it was dark.

The bad thing about a relationship like we had was that you could never get enough, it was an addiction. That is probably the reason her husband became suspicious and tracked me down. He let me know, on no uncertain terms, while recklessly waving a 38 special – (pistol) in my face, that I was trespassing. And that his wife's voluptuous body might be the death of me.

I fixed us both a glass of ice water and brought along an extra glass filled with ice cubes. I knew we would probably use them either in the water or on our bodies. While taking a couple sips of cold water and catching my breath a little, I said, "Now might be a good time for you to tell me what the hell you're doing here, other than you had this overwhelming desire to drive 140 miles just to give me the best loving I would ever have."

She looked up at me with that mouthing motion of a kiss and without saying a word, told me exactly what I wanted to hear. And at the same time knowing the seed of excitement had been replanted from the unexplained.

By me not knowing whether the next knock on my door, would be a friend or a jealous husband with a 38 special, added to the excitement of the pleasures at hand. All I wanted to think about was enjoying Andrea's beautiful body. At that moment I grabbed her 38's and began to massage them vigorously against what I know must have been the largest hard-on I had ever had in my life to that point. Backward and forward, enjoying every slippery slide through her cleavage. The rock-a-bye-booby-baby-rumble was getting to the point of kum-blazing her chin. Being as sexually astute as Andrea was, she tilted her head and opened her mouth, adding even more excitement to the flavor and sensation of that slippery slide. Then like it was a move we had been practicing for years, she flipped,

I flipped, we reversed positions and she gobbled as I tenderly tongue traveled her tantalizing twat>{{{To the top of the Taurus trait}}} a 69'er. Nothing could be finer than eating from her diner, unless of course, she puts an ice cube in your hiner!!! "Oh, happy day"

She knew what I knew, both of us with ice in hand, began to cool the anal glands; the calming coolness of an ass-hole full of ice, delivered excitement with a slice of spice; once insertion had been complete, an orgasmic eruption we did secrete!!!

I knew I was in heaven. I am not being sacrilegious. I equate many of my experiences to biblical stories. There was King David, King Solomon, Best Sheba and Herod Sodom and Gomorrah. Then there where the two daughters that had sex with their fathers so the family seed could continue. They had to get their father inebriated in order to achieve their objective. I will not try to justify, it makes no sense, why should I. One thing I learned a long time ago there are two people that really know. You cannot fool them, they know the truth. You cannot lie to "God", and you know what you do.

I opened a new chapter in our relationship, when I had never pursued before. As we were slipping apart, I kissed her feverishly and slapped her ass with might. I don't know why I did, but I'm glad I did. We slipped immediately into the most violent lovemaking performance I have ever given, and I am sure the same is true for Andrea. There was biting and scratching, double penetration, insertion of ice cubes, more penetration the sheets were totally saturated, we were, slipping and sliding in loves juices and sweat. About the time I thought my cock was going to explode Andrea force-fed two fingers up my ass, and I delivered a-mother-load. At the very same time her love gate opened. The silky smoothness of her love fluids flooded my esophagus, my tonsils were floating, but I refused choking. There was just no way, I was ready to play, and determined to outlast this voluptuously scrumptious piece of ass.

CHAPTER 11

Sister Love

Suddenly there was a knock on the door. I disengaged immediately and my feet hit the floor. All I could think of was, who the hell is this? Andrea solved it all with a kiss. And said, "Don't worry, I'll get it, just put on some clothes. It's got to be somebody we both know."

I'm thinking, oh boy, I know her husband, her mother and father, and Paula. She slipped into her clothes and went to the door, and as she opened it turned and said, "Are you ready for more?" I looked up and Paula walked in. I didn't know if this was the beginning or the end. The one thing I learned that I didn't understand, this rendezvous was something they planned. I was not exactly sure what to say.

Paula solved that problem for me. She said, "I figured it was time to let you know what the favor I wanted was." Then Andrea broke in with, Paula, what a beautiful outfit that is. Where did you get it?" That's when I knew the ice had been broken and they were both on the same page.

A page that I had never thought about turning before, but it sure as hell sounded like it might be fun, so I said, "Alright, let's get to it."

But it was not that easy, as I would soon find out. Paula responded to her sister's question about her outfit then turned to me and said, "Get dressed Brent, we need to take a ride."

She must've read the look on my face because she said, "I know, you thought we were just going to fall right into a menage a trois. Sorry, that will have to wait. We're going to do a little barhopping. I have two auditions later this evening and the first one is in a little club called the M and M bar and grill in Indianhead Maryland." I said, "That's great, where is the next one?" She replied, "The Bar J Ranch, it's a really nice honky-tonk, and much larger than the M&M club. It is located between Waldorf, and the Laplata, Maryland on route 301, down in southern Maryland." Paula continued with, "It's a little farther down towards the eastern shore than Waldorf, you've heard of Waldorf haven't you Brent." I sure had, and I nodded my head yes. Although, I had no idea where Indianhead or Laplata was, and quite honestly didn't give a damn.

I was with two unbelievably gorgeous and sexy sisters, that seemed like they were getting their rocks off by subjecting me to their seductive mannerisms. However, I did feel from the way Paula asked me about Waldorf, she may have been holding something back for later conversation. I indicated to her I would be ready in a jiffy and asked, "Are we going to stop by Waldorf for a few minutes? I like those slot machines." Paula came back with, "Oh you do, do you, I hear their addictive." And I will say for sure, if every time I play the slot machines I end up in the same situation as the last one, they would become a very welcome addiction.

In a few minutes we were already to leave. But first Paula had to stop at the front desk and tell the manager she would be off from work for a few days because her sister was down for a visit. Then she looked at me and said teasingly, "We are going to take my car, it's got more room for Brent to get lost in. And who knows we may pick up somebody."

Paula drove a1958, or 59 Chrysler 4-door sedan, it was a pretty big car. I opened the back door and started to get in but Andrea grabbed my hand and said, "No Brent, you get the fun seat, front and center." So I got in the front-seat between her and Paula. I know a lot of guys wouldn't like that, but I was exactly where I wanted to be.

We where driving across the Wilson bridge into Maryland on interstate 495. Andrea put her hand on the inside of my thigh and said, "Brent, you took driver education, didn't you?" I nodded my head yes and she continued. "Do you remember what the nick-name for the middle seat in front is?" I replied, "No I don't, I was the only boy in class, and I sat in every seat in the class at least once." It was a good thing I knew how to drive before I took driver ed, because I did not learn anything about driving. I could barely remember my name after class was over. She gave my leg a little squeeze just above the knee, and rather sensuously whispered, "They call it the suicide seat, because more deaths can be attributed to the middle seat occupant of the front if they are involved in an accident." I immediately placed my hand on Paula's right thigh and said, "Oh Paula, I was such a fool, please drive carefully, don't try to teach me now, what I should have learned in school." Paula laughed a little and Andrea poked me gently in the ribs, and I said, "Besides, I've got a lot of loving to do." But if I have to go, what a way to go, between the two of you."

As we were pulling into the parking lot at the M&M bar and grill and Paula said, "Give me a kiss for luck." So I did, and I guess I overdid it a little because Andrea tapped me on the shoulder and said, "She said for luck, not fuck." She was smiling when she said it, I guess she was kidding.

As we were walking in the club Andrea gave Paula a little sisterly love hug and said "Show-em how it's done baby." Paula walked on up to the band area and I guess started talking to the bandleader. I told Andrea, "You don't have to worry about your sister she sings really well." She said, "I know that, and I'm not worried. Paula can get a job with any band she wants to sing with." I asked Andrea if she knew what Paula was going to sing. She indicated that she did not but that she knew every song out there.

Andrea and I walked around and found a table then sat down and ordered drinks. I thought this would be a good opportunity to find out what made Andrea come to visit her sister at this particular time. I had only been gone from that area about a week. I said to her, "Andrea, I hope you don't take this the wrong way, but is there something I should know about the reason for your sudden appearance?" She took a drink and a drag off a cigarette and said, "I left the son-of-a-bitch." I shockingly asked, "Why, he has a lot of money. He can give you anything you want. Why would you leave him?" Andrea began to open up a little and said to me, "You have no idea, because you provided the good times. I had to put up with the bad times. Thank "God" we had no children. I never told you about the violence, I never told you about the abuse, because you were my outlet. You are the one I look to for happiness and love." I thought, oh shit, am I ready for this. I was having too much fun to be under the gun.

She must have noticed that I was not taking that information well. She said, "Paula is getting ready to sing, let's talk about something else. We can discuss this later." But I couldn't help myself, so I asked, still thinking about the gun that had been waived in my face. "Where is he?" She very quickly replied, I do not know, nor do I give a damn. Paula is singing now so listen."

And wouldn't you know, the title of her first song was, Your Cheating Heart." Paula's audition apparently included the whole set. Her next song was, Honky-Tonk Angel. It was like she knew what we were talking about, because her whole repertoire directly related to our situation. She did one hell of a job on everything from Night-life, to I Can't Stop Loving You. Then Paula, very dramatically, ended her performance with, Pledging My Love, by Johnny Ace. I thought it was kind of an unusual song to end with when you are performing in a honky-tonk. But Paula knew what she was doing, the way she sang it would draw a crowd on any street corner. Although, I wish it would have been, Dream Lover. Because that is what Andrea really was. And that's the part I was training to prepare for in the dream-world I wanted my life to become.

I was not sure where I could take this relationship. I knew it was going to cramp my style regardless of what I did. I loved Andrea, with a love that was immeasurable, but I also loved Paula, and Becky, with that same desire to love and be loved. Have an easy desire to please and be pleased, with the satisfaction of knowing, and understanding the art of making love. While providing persuasiveness for the ultimate pleasures by pressing loves limits.

I was unable in my mind to differentiate true love from fantasy, nor did I want to. Why did it seem so hard for me to come to terms with love's influences? I love Andrea, I love Paula, I love Becky, I only kissed Sandy, and I love Sandy. I was only 20, was I just in love with love?

Is this going to be a situation that I cannot escape without hurting someone? The problem I have always experienced when I hurt someone is that it hurts me more than it does them. These thoughts were weighing heavily on my mind.

Then with no warning, Paula grabbed my hand and said let's dance. Her audition was over and apparently, she could tell that mine and Andrea's conversation was in trouble, so we danced. As I held Paula close she rubbed that very special set of 38's against my chest and said, "Relax, you don't have to marry her. Just make her happy, and by doing so you will make me happy. And for that I will supply you with more happiness than you ever thought you could have. Because I know, not only what is in your heart, but what is on your mind. You and I Brent are two of a kind. Andrea lives in a fantasy world. Fulfill her fantasy and I will make your wildest dreams come true." She kissed my cheek gently and said thank you.

Within minutes we were on our way to Laplata, Maryland and the Bar-J Ranch. It seemed like it took forever before I saw a sign that said Waldorf. And before I could say, let's stop for a minute Paula said, it's 10:45 the Bar-J closes at 2 AM. This place stays open all night. And besides, the friends I'm hoping to run into here, are all-nighters. You know two, three, four, and five a.m.'er's. They are like vampires. They cannot stand the light of day. We'll stop here on the way back. Hey, she was in charge, like I said before, I was happy in the middle.

It was only a couple minutes before things started heating up in the front seat. I guess Andrea thought I was getting bored. She turned slightly towards me put her hand on my leg, leaned over and kissed me on the cheek. In less than a second we engaged in a lip-lock from heaven that lasted almost all the way to the Bar-J, which was only about 10 minutes away. Andrea had handily gestured my cock and kept me in hard-on status. The seatbelt law was

not in effect at that time so I guess we must have gotten a little out of our regular positions. Paula said, "Alright you guys, relax this mood a little. We are almost there and you're playing with my mind. Remember, I'm the one that has to be on stage in a couple minutes." Very reluctantly we respected her wishes.

Although I knew, and I believe Andrea knew as well. Paula was just itching to turn this into a three-way. That made me wonder if they were like this with other men. But I really didn't care, I had been brought up in the mindset that everyone should love everyone and be happy. And that's exactly what I intended to do with my life.

We pulled in and parked in the parking lot. There were no parking spaces marked off because it was a dirt-gravel parking lot. Unfortunately, mother-nature had delivered a drizzling dampness to settle the dust. So we had to be a little careful where we stepped.

After I paid the cover charge and we walked in Paula and Andrea went to the ladies room. It seemed to like they were gone forever, and it felt like everybody in the place was staring at me. They either saw the two gorgeous young ladies I walked in with, or they thought I was out of place. They all dressed a little differently than I. Most of them were wearing cowboy hats with boots and jeans. I, of course, three-piece suit and tie with my patented patent leather shoes. So maybe I was a little out of place.

When the girls finally returned to take care of me, they seemed a little upset that I had not got a table. I apologized and waved at the waitress. She came over and led us to a table. Paula told her what she was there for and the waitress responded with oh yes, Floyd has been waiting for you. I'll let him know you are here. Paula said to her, "I would like to have a drink and compose myself, so if you would tell him where I'm sitting and to come by on his next break that would be nice."

The waitress nodded okay and as she walked up to the bandstand, I guess she was writing a note, because she handed something to the singer. He looked back towards us and waved. It was only a few minutes until he accompanied us at the table. He pulled another chair over and sat down then introduced himself. He seemed like a pretty nice guy.

I found out later that he was originally from Texas and had been on tour with several of the big country music stars. Entertainers like Carl Smith, Webb Pierce, Faron Young, cowboy Copas, and Lefty Frizzell. Floyd apparently, had not climbed the ladder of fame high enough to enjoy the same success as some of the others. He retired and left the touring behind. He bought a honky-tonk and put a barbershop out back where he worked part-time as a barber.

He had his entertainment pretty well organized. There was no downtime from live music. Every third set and between set breaks were done by a backup band. Each night he had three different backup bands, and this was the last one of the evening. The main band, which was his band, would finish off the night. I believe the term they used was, take it home. In a few minutes Floyd stood up and said, "Paula we have about 25 minutes left on break. Let's go to the band room so I can introduce you and we can organize your set."

As she stood up we held her hand and said, "You got it baby." Andrea said, "Yeah, it's late and it won't hurt anyone, turn it loose and kick some ass." I guess she knew ahead of time what Paula had planned to sing, because that's exactly what she did. Paula must have had this all worked out with Floyd ahead of time. She even had her change of clothes waiting.

Floyd walked out on the stage to open the set with a little Bayou song called the "Diggie- Liggie-Li". Then he began to tell the crowd that he had a big-big treat for them and introduced Paula, she threw open the curtains on the back of the stage and came busting out, and I mean "bustin'" out to where Floyd was standing. The crowd was already making a lot of noise, especially the guys. The wives and girlfriends were mostly taking a deep breath. Some were smiling and clapping, some looked and acted like they were in shock. I looked over at Andrea and could not help myself, I said, "Jesus Christ she's gorgeous, I could eat her alive right on that stage." Andrea looked at me with a sort of sexy I'll kick your ass smile and said, "You lucky bastard, don't make promises you can't keep. This is only the beginning. Before this night is over you will have to perform. And you will be really lucky if you live to see the morrow."

I heard every word she said, and it all sounded good to me, but right now I was stuck like glue to Paula's appearance on stage. She had long dark brown almost black hair and was wearing a cowgirl hat, cocked up a little in the front. They must have poured her into the sweater and jeans, then dressed her down with a pair of designer cowgirl boots. Paula very sexually accented it all with a long hot-pink silk scarf wrapped around her waist and tied in the front. It was hanging down in the shape of a perfect upside-down pyramid. It had been starched or sewn into place for the purpose of exposing while announcing her femininity and accentuating the obvious possible points of interest.

The crowd was still quite noisy when Floyd said, "It's all yours baby, take it away." He handed her the mic, she walked up a little closer to the edge of the stage, kind of bent over a little so everyone could see there truly was a Valley Of The Dolls. Paula was letting them know that her 38's were not being holstered, then said, "How y'all doin' tonight?"

More applause erupted and I looked over at Andrea and said, "Baby, I see a lot of horny guys and unhappy gals, I just hope we don't have to fight our way out of here. Hell, I only weigh 145 pounds. Some of these women could beat the crap out of me. And most of the men look like mountains. Maybe I should leave now." Andrea was laughing as she replied, "You worry too damn much, so have a drink and enjoy yourself while you can. Just remember what I said and look forward to what this night holds in store for you." I motioned for the waitress and told her to bring me a shot of wild Turkey with a beer chaser. Some people call it a boiler maker. All I knew was that Paula's boiling money-maker was making my blood boil and I needed a boiler maker to keep my body parts in check, hell, it might take two or three.

Paula opened her performance by walking out around the front of the stage which was kind of shaped like a half-moon. She directed her comments to the ladies and told them, this one is for all you girls that know your daddy is doing you wrong and can't catch him doing it, and she said, "Just remember, what goes around comes around, in time it all comes back around. And if it's true, remember this." As she lead right into her opening song, Your Cheating Heart. Then she changed up on them before they got off the dance floor, with her version of a Webb Pierce hit called Honky-Tonk. Before they could catch their breath, she had them slow dancing again to Patsy Cline's, Crazy. After which she gave them a couple minutes to relax and have a drink. While she was finishing up her audition, or, performance Andrea and I danced to a couple songs. We talked a little while and I helped my mind and body to two more boilermakers.

The crowd appeared to be very cool and seemed to like Paula a lot. It was getting close to the end of her performance and she called Floyd to the mic with her to thank him personally for the opportunity that he gave her to audition. Then she said, "Floyd, you and I have known each of for quite some time, and you know that if I owe somebody a favor I try to pay or return that favor. I know you feel the same about favors as I do. There is someone in this crowd that I consider a friend who has owed me a favor for a while." I looked over at Andrea and said, "I think she's talking about me. What the hell is she up to?" I could tell she knew by the look on her face as she replied, "I wouldn't have any idea, that's between you and her." My thoughts went back to Paula and Floyd at the mic as she continued by saying to him, "I wonder if I could impose upon you and your band to help me collect that favor. I know he is just dying to get even with me right here and now." I glanced quickly at Andrea and said, "Your sister is crazy if she thinks I'm going to sing dressed in a three-piece suit in front of this crowd." She came back with "So, take your jacket off, then you will only have a two-piece." I looked at her and could tell she and Paula had cooked this shit up together. Then Paula said to Floyd, "It is my understanding that this guy can sing. I have never heard him, but I would like to hear him tonight. Would you do me a favor, which means I will owe you one, and call him up for me?" Floyd responded with, "I sure will baby, what's his name?" She told him my name and he said, "Brent, it sounds like you better get your ass up here. I know I wouldn't keep this lady waiting, and neither should you if you know what's good for you." I killed the last part of my drink stood up and took off my jacket. I looked over at Andrea and she winked with a sheepish little smile. Then I proceeded to make my way to the stage.

Although the crowd was nice, some of them applauding, I tried not to make eye contact with anybody. As I walked up to the mic I shook Floyd's hand. Paula reaches deep into the left side of her mostly topless sweater and pulled out a little piece of paper. As she handed it to me she said, "I would like to hear these, and I know you know them." I took the paper then pulled her in a little closer and kissed her on the cheek by the ear as I whispered, "You beautiful little bitch. I'm going to tear you a brand-new ass tonight." She smiled and told me, "Unbutton your vest an loosen your tie, relax a little and have fun." Then Paula squeezed my hand and left the stage. As I stepped up to the mic, I unbuttoned my vest and the top button of my shirt. Then loosened my tie while reading what Paula had written. Other than her requests she wrote, "I have kept this note close to my heart all the time I was singing, so put your heart in it. Two hearts together cannot lose. Perform well and your reward will be something all men dream of but very few receive." I reached out and took the mic off the stand then move the stand over to the side a little. Then I addressed the crowd with, "Sorry about that, I was totally unprepared, and Paula took advantage of me. But that's okay she can take advantage of me anytime she wants to. These next three songs are her favorites, so if you will bare with me I will try to please Paula. How about that girl, isn't she great?" At that very second the band broke into the first song written on the note, which was, Take These Chains From My Heart And Set Me Free. That verified my suspicions that this had been a total set up. Running through my mind while the band was making their intro was, alright, I'll give it my best shot and look forward to my reward. The next one naturally had to be Elvis. Everybody sings Elvis and his Teddy Bear. Then she had finished me off with Buddy Holly's, Oh Boy.

I thanked the crowd and the band, shook hands with Floyd again and left the stage. The applause was overwhelming, I had a standing ovation. And on my way to the table 3 young ladies came up to get my autograph. When I arrived at the table I put my jacket on, buttoned my vest and straightened my tie then sat down and said, "So there, take that and smoke it in your pipe." Paula and Andrea were both clapping. They stood up and came over to my chair, one on either side. As though it had been rehearsed, in unison they bent down and kissed my cheeks. Then throwing their hands in the air and applauding more, as did the rest of the crowd they both looked at me and motioned for me to get up. At which time, the crowd got louder. So, I stood up and waved then took somewhat of a bow. I motioned for the waitress and ordered another boilermaker.

We all sat down and things got a little quieter. Andrea reached over and put her hand on my hand and said, "You are really good." At almost the same time Paula grabbed my other hand and said, speaking of pipes, where did you get those pipes?" I smiled and leaned over a little closer to her and replied, "From orally massaging boobies and eating pussy." While still holding my hands they both grabbed each other's hands, and everybody squeezed agreeably. Then while they were closer, I whispered to them, "Since this is a day for collecting favors and promises, I'm looking forward to collecting my promises from you both. While we are on the topic of pipes, I'm kind of in the mood for some pipe cleaning too."

The waitress brought my drink and handed me a card and said, "This person wants you to call them sometime.

The rest of your drinks have been paid for." I tried to get her to show me where they were, but she told me they wanted to remain anonymous tonight. I asked her if she got a chance to please thank them for me. I put the card in my wallet and got back to Paula and Andrea's attentiveness.

CHAPTER 12

"*A Motorized Menage a trois*"

It was almost 1:30 a.m. when we decided to head back toward Waldorf. Paula had the least to drink so she was still driving. I climbed back into my little suicide seat, and as we pulled onto the highway, I began to enjoy the treasures and pleasures promised by both sets of 38's earlier that evening. We had not gone much more than a mile before I decided it was time for me to start collecting the totality of my rewards. It was not that I didn't want to pay attention to Andrea, but it was like I was being controlled by a demanding impulse to handily pursue Paula. Since she was driving, I just naturally thought it would be nice if I paid more attention to her. Thank "God" she had got out of that skin-tight outfit she had been singing in, otherwise my play time would not have been half as enjoyable and quite possibly frustrating for both of us. I knew it was only a few minutes to Waldorf. I wanted to show my appreciation in any way I could as I slipped my hand up in Paula's bra-less boob-haven and serviced her titty's, with a gentle nipple pinching process. Her nipples achieved hardness immediately and she shifted her seating position a little. I certainly did not want to interfere with her ability to steer the car, so I dropped my hand to her inner thigh. It became obvious that she came prepared to pay up on her promises. Paula was ready and willing and not wearing a bra or panties. I very quietly said, "Alright, easy access everywhere." She whispered, "I thought you'd like that."

Then suddenly Andrea said, "What are you guys doing?" I told her I was starting to collect my reward. She leaned forward a little and could see by the lights on the dash exactly what was happening. She said whiningly, "I want to play too." Paula began to squirm a little and in doing so made finger fucking more available. I could tell what she wanted so I pulled out and reinserted each finger individually several times into her pussy. She began to move vigorously in her seat. By this time Andrea had unzipped my pants and was rather hurriedly jerking me off. Having all my fingers and right hand totally saturated with Paula's love juices, I removed it and replaced it with my left hand. While doing so I took my forefinger stuck it in my mouth and sucked all the juices off. Paula began surrendering a series of squirms for desire, so I put the middle finger of my love juice saturated hand to her lips. She immediately began slurping and sucking on each individual finger and my hand until all juices were gone. At just about that same time Andrea had decided to suck my cock. That's all it took, I went off like a rocket, or maybe two or three rockets. Paula could tell by my actions what was happening and said, "I want some," Andrea, being a loving sharing sister, started rubbing her fingers around the head of my prick until they were covered with kum. Then she moved her fingers toward Paula's mouth and with a caring, almost baby-talk tone she said, "Here you go baby, some of Brenty's kum for Paula." I could hear Paula's hungry licking, sucking, slurping sounds on Andrea's fingers and hand. Paula's neck began to tighten and her whole body moved a little. I immediately started a rapid-fire insertion rhythm with my middle finger into her pussy. And at the same time, while she was sucking my cock, Andrea had positioned her butt so I could have easy entrance with my right hand to her twat.

Andrea had become very juicy from the excitement of everything that had been going on. With lubrication readily available I could see no reason not to take advantage of an agreeable three- way orgasmic discharge. I knew Paula was almost there, and I could kum again at any time. I rubbed some juices around the opening of Andrea's pretty little prune, while lubricating my thumb. I think Paula had already had two or three more mini-orgasms, but I wanted her to have the big one, and I knew she did too. So I started working my left hand and fingers a little faster in and out of Paula's pussy. She was increasing her body movement in response to me, while I'm whispering, "Yeah baby-yeah baby, yeah baby, do it now, do it now-now-n-o-w do it." Paula is moving, I'm moving, Andrea is moving, love is moving the three of us in unison. As I entered Andrea's tight little ass-hole with my thumb I said, "It's time to Kum-Kum-Kum, Kum baby, Kum, Kum baby, Kum, work it now, work it now, work it, work it, work it. It was so unbelievably spontaneous. It was like a volcanic eruption. As soon as I popped that little prune with my thumb in Andrea's butt-hole, she put a lip-lock on my cock with a high-powered vacuum cleaner suction. I thought she was going to suck my balls right through my prick. I came, she came, Paula came, and all at the same time Paula pulled off the road and through the car in park before it was even stopped and started kissing me. Andrea was kissing me. I was kissing them, and they were kissing each other. Everybody was eating pussy, sucking cock, tongue, and nipples. I was expecting the car to backfire at any time. I know I was glad Paula had that big "ole" Chrysler. I don't believe we could have managed that in my Chevy, the seats were too small. Paula was trying to get to my cock, so I slid over a little toward the door somewhat on my side. She started sucking my cock and said, "I feel like biting this damn thing often take it home with me." While sitting on my face Andrea interrupted and said, "No, no, I found it first, it's mine. I want it Sis." All while she was slithering down under the steering wheel and licking her sister Paula's pussy. I had another nut-buster just thinking about the sister-love going down in the front seat of that car. Paula took all my juices and rubbed it through her hair and all over her face. She was having little mini-orgasms and shaking as though she was about to explode. Andrea came again in my mouth. the whole car smelled like love potion.

I wish Polaroid cameras had been invented back then. I sure would like to have a picture of us in our tightly tangled twat and cock sexually satisfying little love nest, other than in my mind. You had to be involved in order to appreciate and believe what truly happened. There was nothing left for the imagination every bodily orifice and protrusion point had been pleasured and pleased or sanctioned and satisfied.

We stopped for a minute just to make sure the car was clear off the road. Fortunately, it was, although there was not very much traffic at that time in the morning and nobody around.

We were all outside standing around the front of the car while Andrea was smoking a cigarette. I just couldn't take it any longer, I told Paula, "Set your tight little ass up on that hood and lay back. You prepared a perfect chamber of mental misery in my mind. My tongue has been stiff, and my prick has been hard ever since you walked out on that stage. Andrea, feel free to do whatever comes to mind, I'm fine with everything. But you know I have been wanting to eat Paula's pussy ever since she performed her modeling talents with that sexy outfit earlier this evening. You, my dear Paula, are going to remember I was here. I'm going to eat you so good you will always remember. Hell, I might just tear you a brand-new ass-hole before I am finished devouring your scrumptiousness. I put my hands around the back of her tight little butt and pulled her pussy up against my lips. Andrea had started a serious suction-cup nipple-extraction process on Paula's tits. I caught a little glimpse of that and got more excited and lost more love juice. I was gently massaging her little clitoris with my tongue, Andrea was sucking her tip. Paula was trying to reach Andrea's body, so Andrea climbed up on the hood beside her and Paula started finger fucking her. I could feel bodies moving so I glanced up and Paula was licking Andrea's pussy and trying to reach her tits.

What a creatively gorgeous picture of sex was coming together on the hard-hood-bed of that big "ole" Chrysler. If Rembrandt or Michael Angelo could have captured that moment it would have gone down in history as a work of art.

It seemed like we just kept **kumming and kumming.** I was glad I was where I was, because Paula always had an overflow of love juices sweeter than honey. Her diet must consist of a lot of sweets, she sure has some sweet meat, and treats.

We were on our way to Waldorf, which only turned out to be three or four minutes away. As we pulled into the parking lot of the Wigwam bar, Paula looked at me and said, "You are one crazy little lovemaking son-of-a-bitch. It's no wonder Andrea left her husband." I said, "Baby, I'm just getting started, I like the way y'all make love. Why don't we just get a room, take our luggage up and order some room service. A couple bottles of champagne and make a night of it, I'll pay."

She then informed me the rooms had already been taken care of, she said. "We are in room 222 and 223, they are connecting rooms." I ask her, "Why do we need two rooms?" She replied, "Oh, there are several reasons, and they're nice to have in case we do need them." Andrea jumped in with, "I thought you wanted to play the slots." I replied, "Honey, the slots cannot compare with what y'all got. I vote we stay in our room and let love blossom and bloom."

Paula insisted, "You two take the luggage, I will pick up the key and meet you at the rooms. And we will decide from there." I don't know why I felt there was something I wasn't being told about. I had felt like that all along, and I was right once. All I could say is if it would be anything like it has been so far this afternoon and evening, I would welcome it with open arms and a hard-on.

When Paula arrived with the keys we had already been there probably five minutes. Just another reason for me to think something's up. She unlocked the door to room 222 and we took ourselves and our luggage in.

My eyes got stuck on the bed, so I immediately positioned myself in a horizontal position and dropped my suitcase, while at the same time screaming, "Come on baby, bring me some luck, I was born to fuck. We are in a gambling joint and we can hit the slots after I hit you're twats." There was no response, but I heard the door to the next room open. As I sat up, they were closing the door, then I heard a click. I thought, "Oh shit, I must have pissed them off." I got up walked across the floor and was about to knock on the door when they informed me, they were going to take a shower and would be ready in a few minutes. I thought that sounded like a pretty good idea. Although, I hated to part with all the lovemaking aromatic explosions that were being released from my entire body and stinglingly igniting my senses, including my lips and tongue.

I reluctantly got undressed and jumped in the shower. When I finished, I took a couple towels, dried my hair and walked over to the bed and laid down on the towels. I must have dozed off for a moment, because when I opened my eyes it all began again. The only thing different this time was, **we were all *Naked,*** which only added to the excitement. Paula and Andrea's bodies were mostly identical. If it were not for their face and hair, I would have thought I was fucking the same lady or having hallucinations. This also added to the excitement, because in my mind, thoughts were building about how in the hell I happened to be fucking lucky enough to fall into a twin-sexton-sister situation that seemed to be surviving only for the pleasure of sexually satisfying me in every way possible. Or, should I say, having orgasm after orgasm through the never-ending Art of making love.

As we slithered and slipped through numerous accountings of orgasmic interludes, one thing became very obvious to me. There was nothing, and I mean nothing, more gratifying or satisfying, than a complete day of sisterly satisfied lovemaking. They were truly a duet I will never forget.

By the time we arrived on the scene at the wigwam's casino arena it was almost 4:30 AM. The place was packed. Live entertainment was still going on. It looked like all the card tables, slot machines, or one-armed bandits were occupied. I told the girls I was going to try to find a table close to the bar.

I found the waitress and she put our names on the waiting list. Then she told me to find something to do for entertainment and they would call my name over the loudspeaker when the table became available. I asked her if I could get a drink to walk around with. She told me sure and asked what I wanted. I told her a bottle Black label. She made a speedy return with a cash register ticket for $1.50 I gave her two bucks, took my beer and went looking for Andrea and Paula.

When I finally found them, they were at the controls of a one-armed bandit. Much like their lovemaking habits, they enjoyed doing things together. They both inserted the coins and pulled down the stick at the same time. That broke my mind and sent it on a trip of comparison. One of which was, wouldn't it be awesome if they could both jerk me off, a little double handed action. Now with my mind in overdrive the next step would be a dual action blow job. Not only could I feel it, but I could see it. All of a sudden, I had this warm feeling in my stomach.

I started smiling and walked up to them and said, "You ladies do everything very well together, and make it look so sexy. You have no idea what I'm thinking right now." Paula replied, "Oh yes we do." Andrea interrupted with, "And we are going to make it all come true, just for you."

About that time my name came over the loudspeaker. I told them the table was ready and we needed to go before they gave it to somebody else. Together they screamed, "No, we want to practice for a while." I asked, "Practice for what?" Andrea replied, "Practice makes perfect, you go back to the table and when we become perfect, will find you. Then maybe we can get a little bite to eat." I nodded approval but at the same time was thinking, they know damn well what I want to eat. I guess it had probably been a half hour to 45 minutes, I know I had two more beers by the time they walked up and sat down. I ordered them a drink and then said, "Well, have you gorgeous young ladies achieved perfection?" They shook their head yes and looked at each other and smiled. I had no idea what they were smiling about but I knew for sure something was up, something I knew absolutely nothing about, and quite honestly did not give a shit. I said, "I have no idea why you were worried. It is my professional, but humble opinion, your efforts were futile since you were both already holding perfection status."

The only thing I really cared about was looking forward to losing about 20 pounds and having my body turn into, as the saying goes, eyeballs and ass-hole. In other words, attempting to fuck myself to death. Or have as much sex as I could in as many different ways as possible, while learning all the ins and outs and angles of the trade.

The way it seemed so far with these two sisters, there were no limits or boundaries. So, I just might be able to accomplish my goal. Also rolling around in the back of my mind were the original thoughts of what was Andrea doing here. Under the circumstances of the way the stage was being set, lead me to believe there was no way she was here to create an up-tight together relationship with me. I was perfectly fine with that idea.

I knew I was young, but from what I had seen in my short lived love and life experience's I could confirm that friends make better lovers than lovers make friends. Unless you have made that total commitment, which was the farthest thing from my mind. Jealousy is always present in a lover's relationship, but not so much so in a friendship. I want nothing to do with a relationship that's filled with jealousy, they can turn deadly. I have been surrounded a couple times with the jealousy scenario and have made myself a promise that I would try to stay out of trouble by not infringing on husbandry possessions.

Meanwhile back at the tables and out of my mind, Paula and Andrea had finished the drinks and indicated they would like to get something to eat. I said, "That's fine, where do you want to go?" Paula informed me the breakfast bar at the wigwam was excellent, and that she had tried it before. I told them, "Hey, let's do it, I might need a little more energy for later." Andrea jumped in with, "You might need a lot more and you think, so eat a good breakfast."

There was no bill to pay since you had to pay as you ordered. We finished our drinks then made our way to the breakfast bar. The self-service bar had just been replenished and was starting to get busy. I guess most people there knew when the best time was to frequent the breakfast bar.

I noticed Paula had a few friends she spoke to in the restaurant. That told me she had been there before. While we were eating, I asked them how they came about getting the slot machine. Paula said one of her friends had the machine, but she had something she needed to do and ask her if they would watch her machine until she returned. We finished eating and Paula said, "Wow, it's daylight, we better get upstairs and get some rest, we've got a big day tomorrow, I mean today."

On our way to our rooms, we kind of filtered and mingled through the different gambling areas which were still totally busy. To me it was a little unbelievable, but after all it was the weekend.

Although there were two regular size beds in each room, they insisted that I have a room by myself. At that point I had just eaten, and my mind was a little tired and thought maybe I needed some rest, so I did not object. I didn't even know what room number I was in. I just brushed my teeth got undressed and went to bed. I guess I was more tired than I realized.

CHAPTER 13

My Ultimate Lovemaking Training Program

*****THE FINALE*****

I was asleep when my head hit the pillow. For how long, I'm not sure. I was awakened by a female voice whispering, "Oh shit, Paula must have given me the wrong key." She kept whispering to whomever was with her. As she came closer to the bed I turned over on my right side and partially shaded my eyes from the sunlight that found its way into the room through a window with the blinds not fully drawn. There was no mistaking, I could tell by that larger-than-life hourglass figure, it could only be one person. Just as I started to call out her name, she said, "Oh my "God" it's Brent." She sat down on the edge of the bed. I said, "Baby, please don't wake me. I am in the middle of a two-day dream from heaven and do not wish to have it interrupted.

However, should you choose to become a participant and help prolong a pleasurable ending, please share this stage with me, lay down and let's make love." She replied, "Brent, what the hell you doing here? You are either the craziest, or the horniest little fucker I have ever known. You should still be out there chasing college girls, or high school cheerleaders instead of hanging out with us. For Christ's sake, I'm 10 years older than you are and I know you young guys fall in love too easy. Besides, I'm not interested in becoming your mother."

This must have been what was behind all those little snide remarks and innuendos about Waldorf and wait until tomorrow, that Paula and Andrea had been making. I said to myself, the hell with it, i'm going for it. I threw the cover back, which left me stark naked and my prick was hard as a rock, standing straight up and weeping for attention. Becky's eyes got big and her mouth flew open, as she reached over and grab my cock she said, Damn boy, were you born with a hard on?" I told her I didn't know, I could not remember back that far. But I had been told that I was always showing it off and playing with it. Then I said to her, "It has been like this since yesterday morning. I told you I was in the middle of a two-day dream and in my mind, you became a part of that dream as I saw your form approaching my bed. You will always have an open invitation to my dreams. I have decided I'm going to name one of my pillows Becky."

She had started slow jerking my cock, then bent over to kiss it. As she did, she pulled my foreskin around the head of my cock and licked it back and forth so gently I could feel the roughness in the texture of her tongue. She said, "It's like a mushroom, and I love mushrooms. But right now, I'm looking for a friend of mine named Paula her sister Andrea." I smiled and said, "So am I, they're the ones that started this dream yesterday."

As I reached my hand up to her face, I continued with, "Why don't you have your friend knock on that door right over there, it goes to the next room. While she is becoming acquainted with Paula and Andrea, you and I can examine the possibilities of mushrooms and banana splits for dessert." She gave my pecker one big power suck and a semi bite, then insisted, "No, we are looking for Paula and Andrea. Paula is going to get an ass whipping. She gave me the wrong room key." I inquired, "Is it okay if I watch? Or maybe we could invite them to my room, and we could all rumble together. I could be the referee. I have never been in the same bed with four women. I went skinny-dipping with six girls in high school. It was a lot of fun, but they were too young to know what was going on. By the way, that takes me back to what we were saying before. I do not want to be with younger girls at this time in my life. They don't know what I need to know or do. Hell, they do not even know what they need to know or want to do. Nor, am I looking for a mother, I just want to learn more and I need a good teacher. Y'all are excellent teachers so teach me tonight, actually I should say, teach me today. Y'all know what you want and how to get it and you get right to it. I have learned so much from you and Paula, of course I knew Andrea before I came to this area. I promise you I will go when I have learned what I need to know but until then let me be your boy-toy."

Becky turned to look at her friend, which I thought was Sandy but then I realized it wasn't. Then she looked back at me and said, "Give me five minutes, I will bring Paula in here and let you beat her butt." I was not exactly sure what to think but I nodded okay. I suddenly recalled how Andrea responded when I smacked her on the ass and was hoping it would turn out to be another one of those sister things. Maybe Paula would respond the same way. I just had to wait and see, and that was always the hardest part for me, waiting. Becky and her friend walked over and knocked on the door to the next room. She reached down and turned the knob only to find it had been locked. I could hear them talking but could not make out exactly what they were saying, so I laid back down and tried to re-enter my dream. I only know that I was in need of sleep enough that I had drifted back into dreamland.

Then I heard the door open. As I looked over, I could see it was Andrea. She was dressed in a tiny little see-through pink négligée. She immediately walked over to the window and pulled the curtains tight to shut off the sunlight. Then she turned all the lights off in the room except the one in the bathroom. She pulled the bathroom door about halfway closed, allowing enough light for you to barely recognize a body shape from a distance.

Andrea walked over to the bed and untied her négligée. With a sexy little shiver-shake, allowed it to slide slowly to the floor and said to me, "Becky told us you have a mushroom problem that needs handled. I thought I would see if there was anything I could do to help solve your problem." I responded by reaching up and pulling her down on the bed to me, as her hand found my crotch I said, "Why certainly Andrea my dear, your interest is extremely welcome, eagerly invited, and long overdue. It seems to be, a rather personal, damn near two-day problem. I am afraid if it lasts much longer it might become eternal." Andrea grabbed my pecker and started laughing. Then she said, "Where do you come up with this shit?"

I started in by kissing her rather feverishly, then devouring her chin, neck, and upper breast. Suddenly slipping into a very selfish nipple-sucking massaging action in the surrounds of a safe-haven provided by the ***Valley Of The Dolls*** for her tits. While at the same time Andrea was inserting all memories of my mushroomed-memorial-cock into her red-hot and extremely well lubricated pussy.

I thought to myself, wow, they must be having a warming up session in the next room. Andrea had been topside, so I rolled her over to the normal, so-called, missionary position and began to calmly release my motor into a reaming the rim process. There was just enough light entering the room to provide visual satisfaction while pleasuring my eyes with her face and body. Andrea was so incredibly gorgeous. She looked absolutely deliciously desirable, and oh, so devourable lying there. Her long blonde hair almost appearing windblown, falling in waves on the pillow, around the sides of her head and down onto her neck and shoulders. She displayed a pleasurably peaceful look of contentment while whispering, "God"

Brent you are so good. Everybody loves you, including me. You're something else, you are all I'll ever want."

Andrea's eyes filled with tears as she lifted her head a little and pulled me down to give me a kiss. For an unconscious moment I thought I was in love. Our bodies began a revolving sort of grinding movement. With my cock still inserted I flipped her lower torso area on its side, she put her left leg over my shoulder. I had positioned my body resting on my knees and straddling her right leg. With my hands wrapped around her hips and her right side I pulled her up in a gentle back and forth revolving motion. My balls were rotating from side to side on her right upper-inner-thigh area. Andrea was lying in a twisted position on her upper back. She was glowing with the satisfaction of love in her eyes. While those taunting tender tears were uncontrollably appearing.

I knew this was Andrea's favorite position for deeper penetration, and she likes it deep, the deeper the better. She had introduced this position to me on our very first sexual encounter. She also insisted on trying this position once on each side to see which one would provide her the most pain-filled pleasure with the deepest penetration. I began a pussy pounding process with all the motor muscle I could muster. Andrea started screaming while scratching my legs and lower back. Then released the moaning and groaning sounds of ecstasy as she started to quiver. I pleasured her vaginal canal with 10 or 15 overdrive motor strokes of pussy pounding, providing deeper penetration on each delivery. With a unified explosion and double shot of our love juices, we collapsed in each other's arms and began kissing. Andrea was weeping as she reached up to touch my face and said, "I love you so much Brent. You have no idea how hard this is for me."

The love juices were still flowing as the door opened and three female figures appeared. With the exception of some towels they were carrying and a few unidentifiable objects in their hands, they were essentially naked. Their faces were mostly shaded from the lack of light.

The only one I did not recognize was Becky's friend and she hadn't introduced us yet. She was very slim and trim. Compared to Becky, Paula, and Andrea she sported very small breasts. Or as later in my life, if I may quote my very special wife. "I'm the president of the Itty-Bitty Titty Committee." Maybe Miss Unknown will consider running for that office.

I have become quite fond of itty-bitty-tittys. Once you bite down on an itty-bitty titty nipple, it cannot beat you up or get away. They are a little harder to titty-fuck while trying to administer an exterior esophagus lube-job. I remember a few years back hearing someone say that more than a mouthful is a waste. I know I damn sure do not agree with that. I love them all, large and small.

As though she had been instructed to do so, Andrea slipped immediately into a multi-level lover mode. She got out of bed and walked over to where they were standing by the door. She seemed to be sobbing a little as she put her arms around her sister. Paula returned the gesture and gave her scrumptious little butt a couple gentle rub-pat and squeeze jobs. It looked kinda sexy, made me wish I was doing it.

They all kind of moved together and formed somewhat of a circle. Becky put one arm around Andrea's shoulder and with the other hand she explored the wetness of the area around her pussy. She then raised her hand towards her mouth and spread her fingers a little, beginning to suck them in a lip massaging manner. She immediately responded with a gentle little kiss to Andrea's lips then dropped her hand to borrow more of the love juices. This time she responded to her unnamed friend in the same manner. Becky slowly slid her other hand around Miss unknown's small breasts and down to her tiny little tummy. Were eventually she started a flat-handed five-finger massaging process on Miss unknowns entire pussy area.

The four of them stood together in a shadow like circle in front of the open door to the next room with a lighted background. It appeared as though they were either discussing their plan of action or consoling each other by hand gestures. They didn't seem to be able to stop touching each other with one body part or another. Sometimes rubbing titties, sometimes hands, sometimes butt areas, and even some leg climbing.

After a few minutes they broke the circle formation and stood side-by-side holding hands in the order of Miss unknown, Becky, Paula, and Andrea. I knew this had to be planned, and planned very well, if I may say so.

I was just leaning up on my elbow watching and going crazy, playing fantasy games in my mind with all kind of desires. I almost started to masturbate but I decided against it due to lack of interest in myself.

Each room was equipped with two double beds. Before I knew what was happening, or could offer to help, they had rolled the other bed right up against the one I was on. Andrea and the unknown lady had folded a blanket and laid it over the area where the two beds come together. At the same time Paula and Becky were locking the wheels in place. I just could not understand how they possibly could have planned this that quickly, so naturally, I thought they had done it before. I must have looked really silly sitting there with my prick in my hand and smiling.

The unidentifiable objects I was speaking of were strategically placed at the very top of the beds and right in the middle for easy access. There were four of them that were still foreign to me. Although I think I could guess what a couple of them might be put into service for, I had never seen any of them before. The only one I kind of recognized looked like it could have been made from a ping-pong paddle. It had several little holes drilled through it and was varnished to a shiny finish. Two of them kind of resembled a penis. One was a little smaller and by itself. The other one looked somewhat like a larger cock and came with a built-in harness attached to a belt. Another was like a short whip with a handle. The small leather straps of the whip had been split and frayed into several tiny little ends maybe as many as 100 or more some of them had been tied in a little knot at the very end. The last one was just some weird looking little machine with an electrical plug, two small hand straps and what looked like a little fan at one end.

What really caught my eye and built my interest is what Becky was wearing. It looked like a belt made of shiny black marbles or beads. Some were larger than others. In the front and the back it had a single strand of the little black shiny balls hanging down about two or 3 feet. This told me she was the dominant force of the four.

I had no idea what to expect or what I was in for, but I knew them all except one and trusted them as excellent love makers. All of this aroused me even more to the point I just could not wait for it to start. As though the look of anxiousness I displayed was their command, it got started.

The first one on the bed was Becky. She sat on a pillow at the head of the bed, right in front of all the tools of the trade. Her legs were almost in a cross, like Indian style sitting. The little black shiny balls were streaming down to a rolled up resting place just below her pussy in front of the pillow. It projected a very sexy appearance and commanded attention. I was still partially laying down leaning on my elbows on the one bed. The next one to break the ice was Paula. She positioned herself spread eagle on her back in front of Becky. Her legs were spread almost halfway on either bed allowing her pussy lips to open, exposing her clitoris for Becky's viewing pleasure. Then came Andrea, after carefully lifting Paula's head she placed a pillow under it. Then leaned over and kissed her on the forehead while teasingly twist pinching both her nipples and said, "You looked so uncomfortable sis." Andrea then got in position on the same bed I was in with her back partially toward me.

Rested her head on its side on Paula's leg just above her knee while finger walking her left hand back and forth between Paula's knee and her pussy. Lastly, the arrival of Miss unknown. She looked so fragile and frail compared to the others. She might have been 5'6" tall and weighed maybe 90 pounds. The rest would go from 110 to130 pounds. She had what you might call, I guess, a female mohawk haircut with a few strands of hair streaming down on both sides onto the back of her neck. She almost looked like a guy.

Then suddenly, I noticed they had all shaved their pussy's. It actually made them appear so much more edible than that of the fur-burgers pussy appeal. I seem to recall picking several pubic hairs out of my teeth after mine and Paula's first interlude.

I could probably have gone to the dentist to get a haircut after that one. But I am sure that was because we had such confined quarters and were really muscling each other in that small little sex shack. I like the shaved pussy effect, it's kind of like you can get to the water without wading through the weeds.

Back to Miss unknown, she, as everyone else, seemed to be very well prompted for her entrance. She walked up to the bed with a semi-manly strut, turned slightly and casually set down on the edge with her hands clasped over her sexy little shaven snatch. Then, all in one slithering slick snake like move Miss unknown became up right standing on the bed. She took one large step to the right and totally covered Becky's upper torso with her body. The next move was unbelievable, it had to be rehearsed. She bent over backwards into a London Bridge formation which placed her cute little cunt no more than an inch from Becky's mouth, and her mouth no more than an inch from Paula's pussy.

This young lady must have been a gymnast and double-jointed. I suddenly felt the seeping sensation of silent coming on the back of Andrea's calf. She must have felt something as well. She very nonchalantly reached back for the head of my cock and with a milking motion cleared my main vein and wiped her calf. Andrea then proceeded to transplant her findings on Paula's breasts.

With not one word being spoken, Miss unknown extended her bridge to encompass Paula's breasts without distancing her pussy from Becky's mouth. In what seemed like an instantaneous reaction, Becky quickly grabbed both of Miss unknown's ass-cheeks with a grip of indentation showing around each finger. Her lips completely covered the little split open hole that hid and held the clit of temptation to her tongue, and then she started a pussy eating procedure that I could only dream of. While at the same time, Miss unknown was tongue-ingly tease-licking my second-hand love liquid from Paula's nipples and the dark brown overlay areas. Her pretty-little pointed pink tongue left a shiny-silk-like trail as it traveled around and around the dark circles at the top points of Paula's tits. My visual reception of her tongue's trail of two-titty's, inspired an electrifying charge to my love muscle. That of course resulted in more of my love lotion on Andrea's lower leg and the nape of her knee. Andrea, while sucking off my leftover treats from her fingers and hand, had perfectly positioned her body under the bridge. There she could assist Miss unknown with her efforts to provide the "boss lady" more pleasure by massaging Becky's clitoris with her tongue. Without neglecting Miss unknown's needs, allowing her butt cheeks to be partially supported by her upper arms, both of Becky's hands found a friendly resting place and Paula's love nest.

With the thumb and forefinger of one hand she spread paula's pussy lips open a little farther than they already were. With the other hand and middle finger, Becky began a very gentle, but masterful, finger fucking massage process on Paula's pussy.

I was in active, so I started rubbing up against and pumping Andrea's leg. She kept moving away and pushing me back with her body. Hell, I was shooting all over everybody. Nobody was paying attention to me except for rubbing in or licking off the orgasmic juices they had all inspired.

To this point we were probably an hour into this lovemaking session, or maybe I should say their lovemaking session. I have shot all over everyone but into no-one. I had four women who were fucking the hell out of each other and driving me freaking crazy. What the hell was going on?

Becky must have seen the look on my face, she looked at me and said, "Brent relax, learn baby learn, you said you wanted us to teach you. When this session is over you will be fully aware of how to please and take care of any woman's needs or desires in the bedroom. Come up and give me a kiss." So I did as she asked and she wrapped her tongue around my tonsils and at what seemed like the precise same time Andrea reached in an attempt to caress my balls. As soon as she touched them, I shot all over the side of her face and Becky's lower body. Hell man, I think I even saturated Miss unknowns bellybutton. Becky, being very careful not to disturb the functions of others, immediately with both hands began collecting the part of my orgasm that landed on her and was energetically rubbing it around on her face and all through her hair.

My thoughts went straight to Paula. She had done the same thing last night. It added more fuel to my suspicion that all of them together had agreed on providing my mind and body with a shock-wave I would never forget. I can very honestly say, I have not forgotten, nor shall I ever forget. Each time those memories reveal themselves it provides me with indescribable chills and thrills. I could have died right there. To tell the truth I probably should have, I was already in heaven.

I had no fucking idea what I was doing. I was in female Crotch-rocket and Firecracker-Heaven. I could bust a nut if somebody winked at me. Andrea was still rubbing my balls softly, and it happened. I yelled out, Jesus Christ and heavenly shit, blow it and damn-it I mean it too." And somebody did. I'm not sure who it was and frankly don't give a damn. I was just happy they did it, at least I got some touch.

I was almost 21 years old before I came to this paradise. I thought I knew my shit, only to find out that when it came to pleasing and making women happy, I didn't know my ass from a hole in the ground. But bound and determined to learn, I stayed aboard that floating in loves juices makeshift double bed boat. At that point, I don't know where the hell in history this came from, but I became Capt. Lawrence and vowed never to give up this ship!

*****(And with that I say good night, I must find something to eat other than memorable pussy's. We are now in the a.m. and there is only one thing I know. Memories are all that is left, for we who live in afterglow. We shall resume right where we left off, just pretend it is intermission and perform your favorite sex act. Go pound a pussy, strap on a dill-doe, masturbate, suck a cock, eat a snatch, tap the nape of your favorite knee, lick the lint out of a belly-button, leave a special little message in someone's armpit, pop a prune, or maybe just a special hug and tender kiss. They are all a part of the art of making love, so don't waste your time. Be back soon. Good night!!!)*****

We are back with a vengeance that overflows with love's juices and surprises. Becky, for whatever reason had decided it was Paula's night to pay the price. She said to me, "This is Paula's birthday and it's her party, have your way." Becky was the "Boss Lady," and it was so obvious, so I obeyed her as everyone else did.

Being as non-disruptive as possible to the many other facets of lovemaking functions that were going on as I could, I mounted Paula in the missionary position. My prick easily accommodated her lubricating needs with a continuous drool, which seemed to have been happening for hours.

Becky reached behind her and picked up the little-short handled whip. Paula and I were flat out making love. We were kissing, moving and grooving and body surfing. I was content just the way things were, but Becky wasn't. She instructed Andrea to strap on the harnessed pecker looking item that now I know as a dill-doe. Becky then told Paula and I to switch positions putting Paula topside. As all this was taking place, Becky was gently lacing and tracing Paula's buttocks and lower back with the whip tales as though she were an artist painting a picture. And indeed, she was playing the part of a great Maestro conducting a multi-orchestrated love-nest ensemble. Becky was manufacturing and putting all the pieces in place to this unbelievably grueling but satisfying love scene. When Paula was securely top-side I became very interested in her nipples. I tried catching one and then the other in a lip lock. Once Andrea was armed and dangerous with the dill-doe, Becky pulled her in closer and gave Miss unknown's pussy a very brief break while kissing Andrea and whispering something in her ear. Then she immediately returned to her past position of passionately devouring the main outlet of Miss unknown's midsection and surrounding condiments. It looked as though Becky was making an attempt to totally swallow her clit. Miss unknown was going crazy, shaking and screaming while violently squeeze- pinching her own tiny little titty's and nipples so hard that immediate redness appeared.

With Paula being taken out of the picture of what once was a perfect London Bridge, Miss unknown was standing like somewhat of a willow in the wind. She was pressing her pussy tightly to Becky's mouth. She had both hands either on the back of Becky's head pulling her face harder and forceful into her love nest, or frantically fondle-slapping her almost non-existent titty's.

Suddenly Becky began to pick up the pace and the force of the whip-slaps on Paula's ass-cheeks and back, while at the same time taking a two-finger dip in Miss unknowns love juice bowl and dropping them quickly to her lips. Becky then decided to deepen my desires for Miss unknown as she slid her fingers and hand up over my lips, nose, and forehead, then into her own pussy. She knew she could tease me with the invitational smell of Miss unknowns secretions. Becky also knew how good it was, she had been putting a bad-ass masterful mouthing-massage on Miss unknown's treasure nest for the last hour. To give me a whiff might heighten my interest in what she had planned for me and Miss unknown's training program later.

Becky had collected a bountiful blessing of her love lava for the lubrication of Paula's ass-hole. On her way to Paula, Becky traced her fingers back down over my nose and lips while motioning Andrea to position her strapped-on friend for entry to Paula's prune. I have no idea how it all took place. What I do know is the dill-doe was larger than my pecker. It must have had lots of lubrication, because with one violent slap of the whip on Paula's ass, Becky had a handful of Andrea's hair and pulled her forward. Paula screamed with a scream that flowed from pain to ecstasy within the same sound. I was positioned perfectly so that it took very little effort for me to perform the courtesy of licking Becky's Kum-twat and sharing it with Paula. Andrea's dill-doe was fully inserted and doing the rub-bounce-boogie off the inner walls of Paula's anal playground.

I became aware of it rubbing on the main vein of my meat. Only being separated by the protective anal/pussy wall that divided Paula's colon from her vaginal canal, Andrea and I were trying to become one. We carefully navigated our love-sticks through the tunnel that was becoming more and more tender to loves touch. We were happy taking this ride together. I think Paula understood, as she pleasured us with a smile.

The feeling of the artificial unconscious cock applying pressure on the main vein of my prick, caused much more than enough friction to build for a maximum performance blast-off. I can't say for sure about anyone else, but I came another 735 times in a row. I think Paula came. I'm not sure, but I think Andrea came, I am positive Becky and Miss unknown came.

Miss unknown's mid-section was hardly visible. Becky's body was totally overwhelming her vagina area. Knowing what Becky's mouth and tongue were capable of, caused me to expect Miss unknown to disappear at any moment. Becky could travel from, cock and balls, to ass and mouth, armpits to elbows, and nipples to bellybutton, then come while she was sucking your toe.

I was truly happy I had followed my uncle Gene's advice and catered to the lady that molested slot machines and made love to one-armed bandits. She was a best teacher and friend I could have ever had. Thank you so very much, you wonderfully gorgeous, seductively sexy Lady, for being a part of my life!!!

We were all five happy and pleasured. I was fucking Paula while occasionally sharing with her the remnants of Becky's pussy. Andrea had served her master by strapping on a dill doe to perform anal entry with the popping of Paula's prune. While Becky was taking great care in the production of this grand performance of sensual and sexual pleasures while personally guaranteeing the pleasures for Miss unknown.

Love and its aftermath was on display for all. Just when I thought nothing else could possibly happen, Miss unknown stood up and reached back behind Becky to pick up the insulated smaller version of a pecker. She inserted it in her pussy then into Becky's mouth, back to her pussy then into Becky's pussy and back to her mouth. Slippery and covered with all the love that was evolving from the nights adventure Miss unknown made a full turn placing her asshole and her clitoris in total submission position for Becky's mouth and it's masterful masturbating tongue moves. Then she stretched her nearly, uncovered naked lanky frame, over all bodies and began to saturate her make-believe prick with Vaseline. Probably because she knew where she was going possibly had never been penetrated before.

I found myself wondering from time to time if Becky was the voice of etiquette for proper pussy eating pleasures. I know she really got into the pussy eating process when it presented itself, regardless of who it was.

While Becky was almost viciously consuming Miss unknowns pussy and ass hole, Miss unknown reached forward and teasingly taunted Andrea's pretty little shiny white rimmed prune. Then much to my surprise, her long and lanky body allowed her the distance needed to reach the orifice of my ass. With gentleness and care along with a lots of Vaseline, Miss unknown popped my prune. Once I felt her there, I knew what was going to happen. What I did not know was what would come next. With the excitement of everything that was going on, such as, the unbelievable sounds of moaning, groaning, and salivating in loves lather. The slipping and sliding while trying to hold positions and bodies together, coupled with the sounds of Becky's eager eating skills while preparing for and craving the consumption of Miss unknown's ass-hole and pussy, became so intensely pleasurable that Miss unknown's body began to violently jerk as she slipped from me to Andrea and back several times which provided a feeling I will never forget. And I have never been satisfied in that manner again. It was like a triple-decker, or maybe I should say a triple-dicker. My dick in Paula's pussy, being massaged by the strapped-on dill-doe that Andrea was wearing. The slender love-stick and unpredictable placing of Miss unknown's hand from the entrance of my ass and Andrea's. The prick of pretense was sliding back and forth, rubbing against my prostate then removed and once again breaching the entrance of Andrea's ass-hole then back to my anal cavity. This started a totally out of control volcanic eruption with everyone climaxing together, and they just kept coming. As their bodies, the tools of their trade, were slipping apart they became semi-motionless resting in each other's arms, hugging and kissing and quite possibly knowing this was a once in a lifetime event.

The last thing I remember before falling asleep, I was eating that sweet tasting skinny little pussy of Miss unknown's while finger fucking Andrea in both her ass-hole and her pussy. Becky and Paula were eating each other and seemingly fighting over who would be next at sucking my cock and balls.

Unbelievable, yes, you had to be there. We all fell asleep in I know what, was the wettest, most slippery and wonderfully satisfying cluster of human flesh I could possibly have ever experienced. And I never have since that day. Oh, how I wish that were not true. Once you learn to love, you never lose the desire or forget the flavor.

The note taped to my chest read, "Brent, when you wake up, and if you're not too tired, your next class will take place either in the bar or the casino. Maybe you should try to get a little bite to eat to replace your energy level, Sweet dreams baby, Becky."??? I was a little puzzled about the note being from Becky and not from Paula or Andrea. I didn't let it bother me there because I knew I needed her. The rest was just icing on the cake. Yes, I was tired, and every muscle in my body was sore. My eyebrows were hurting, and so was my prick. But it was hard as a rock and standing straight up. Just as though it was trying to say, let's go, we've got a diving lesson and I need to get wet.

I brushed my teeth, shaved and showered, threw on another change of clothes and headed for the bar. I had been at the bar about 10 minutes. I finished one beer and helped myself to a couple of the complementary bar snacks then ordered another beer. When the bartender brought the beer he also handed me a note and said, "I think this is for you, or at least you look the part." The note said, "Hangout, be back soon, Becky & Jennifer."

So while I'm drinking my beer I'm thinking, Jennifer must be Miss unknown. But what happened to Paula and Andrea? What about the bartender's comment, is my amateurishtic appearance that obvious? Who fucking cares if it is, I just got out of bed with four gorgeous ladies, performing fantastically unbelievable acts of sex. I bet he wishes he had. As a matter of fact, I bet a lot of people would love to have traded places with me. I wish them well, but in the meantime I say, nanny- nanny-boo-boo, I did what you couldn't do! Probably an uneasy thought of egotism and drunkenness from the night, or day before.

After I finished my beer I ventured out into the arena of one-armed bandits. I got some change so I could play the slots. Then I realized that was a stupid move according to Uncle Gene. He always said, you never use your own money to play the one- armed bandits. But I was a little curious about where all the excitement and enthusiasm was coming from.

It only took about $10 worth of coins before I was about to give up the ghost. Just as I was about to pull the handle on my last coin, I felt a hand in my crotch and one on the handle, and Becky whispered in my ear. "This is how you pull that thing. You've got to have rhythm and timing with sex on your face and sin in your mind." She put her hand on my hand and pulled the handle, and at the same time gave my shank a crank. The machines bells went off and so did I. Becky had lots of fun with that. I could feel her squash-rubbing it against my inner thigh with her hand from the outside of my trousers. I didn't win nearly as much as she did the last time we had enjoyed the slots, but I felt extremely lucky that she had returned to apply her special shank-crank.

I gave her all the winnings, although it only amounted to about $20. To me it felt more like 1 million. The last time Becky thought I was her good luck charm. I didn't have to think, I knew she was my good luck charm and someone I wanted to make sure I kept around forever.

I didn't want to push things, but I was ready to rock. I said to Becky, "Baby I'm wrapped pretty tight, maybe the time is right, I'm ready for you, are you ready for the night?" She started laughing, nodded to the person I now know as Jennifer then said to me. "Don't give me your poetic horseshit, the night is too young. I'm not ready for it, take a walk with me, and keep things light. I'll let you know when the time is right."

Jennifer grabbed a machine and started playing the slots. Becky and I walked out to the parking lot, she led me over to an area that was dark and bent me over backwards on the hood of a parked car. She unzipped my pants and started grooving, when she finished with me, I was barely moving. Becky pulled me up and we straightened our clothes, and then she said, "Listen to me sweetie cause I'm the one that knows. It's only 1030, hell it's not even late, and really good things come to those who wait." I guess she was letting me know that she could put a line or two together as well as I could.

When we got back into the casino and Jennifer was still playing the slot machine. It looked as though couple guys were trying to pay too much attention to her to satisfy Becky. So she walked over to Jennifer, took her by the arm and said, "Come on babe, I got a machine over here I know is ready to go." Just like that, so strange, the mental control she had over everyone. One thing I could tell for sure, Becky was not going to let that pussy get away. From what happened there, I'm kind of surprised she allowed me to eat it the night before.

The next thing I know we are in the dining area having a little sweet snack. I went to the men's room and when I got back it was obvious Becky was explaining to Jennifer the rules of the game. Much like she had explained them to me.

I didn't care what anybody else got, but I got a piece of French Apple pie. Becky immediately informed me that French Apple pie was very sweet and anything sweet was very fattening. Then she said, "Honey, if you are really serious about wanting to do what you say you want to do, you should try to keep your body looking like it deserves to be desired." Becky was giving Jennifer the same advice over a piece of cherry pie and ice cream, while she was helping herself to a very large piece of chocolate cake. I was 5 feet 10 ½ inches tall and weighed hundred and 40 pounds soaking wet. I suppose Jennifer may have been 5'4" to 5'6" if she was lucky, she weighed 95 pounds. While the hand that holds the whip was pushing 6 feet and weighed probably between hundred 130 and 140 pounds. But every ounce of Becky's weight was in the right place. Our conversation went from eats to sweets, two of which, in my opinion are the same thing.

Paula and Andrea, where were they? Becky informed me that Paula got the singing job at the Bar-J and would probably join us later. While in the meantime we would be giving the slots our undivided attention. I jokingly said, "My lovely lady of the night, would it be appropriate if I were to handle you the way you handled me when I was playing the slots?" Becky replied with no hesitation, "Only if you are sure the time is right." She must have been trying to tell me I have a problem with jumping the gun. Which I suppose might be the explanation for several premature ejaculations.

Becky finally found the slot machine she wanted and told Jennifer and I to have our coins ready to occupy the ones on either side when they became available. Finally, we were all three side-by-side, dropping coins and pulling handles. That process continued for what seemed like forever. I know I must have lost about $40 with no return.

They both had probably done the same. When all of a sudden Becky said, "Brent, switch machines with Jennifer, I need you on my right side. I am right-handed and my right hand is a little tired." With no hesitation, the move was made. I wasn't sure what it was all about, I just thought she knew what she was talking about, so I followed instructions. What I hadn't noticed, was that Jennifer was left-handed and apparently didn't have the proper handle pulling rhythm. Becky was not only pulling her handle but helping Jennifer pull hers with her left hand. It was not long until she was working very diligently controlling both hers and Jennifer's machine handles. The body language was taking control. Becky was hip bumping Jennifer with a circular motion, while working her timing out so that at the same time their hips bumped her boobs would rub against Jennifer's shoulder. Becky would, in the same motion, with her hand on Jennifer's hand pull the handles in rhythm.

The eye-movement, the jaw jacking, the head jerking, the lip licking, between those features and the hips and boobs bumping and rubbing Becky was molesting or making love to both Jennifer and the slot machine. With a final body surge and an almost wicked handle pull, the action continued for what must have been about 15 minutes.

It created more and more excitement along the way. I was almost totally neglecting my machine while paying attention to them. I glanced around to some of the other players. Holy shit, it must have been contagious, everyone was doing it.

I dropped another coin, pulled another handle, then another, and another, I felt like that old saying, two is a company and three is a crowd. That thought no sooner crossed my mind than Becky said, with a low drawn out, delivery, "B-r-e-n-t, B-R-E--E-N-T!" That was my signal, the time was right. I had no idea whether Becky was coming, or the machine was coming. I moved over and very aggressively slap- grabbed Becky's pussy area with force. Then implemented a piano playing finger massage on the easy opening lips of her smoothly shaven snatch. When she was about to pull the handle, I squeezed her pussy lips together. When she pulled the handle down, she and the machine had an orgasmic discharge.

One in monetary value, the other in the wetness and moist flavor of loves lava. I'm not sure but I have a feeling Jennifer came. I know damn well I came.

It was something I could not explain. Either she was magic or a witch. For all I knew she may have been electronically wired to the machine. Hell, it might have been all the above. It didn't matter, it happened, and that's what mattered. I felt her pussy muscles tighten when I squeezed, and she gave me a little squirm of approval, then it was over.

We collected Jennifer's coins, went to the bar and ordered a drink. Jennifer's winnings were almost $200. I guess that's not that much, but it was the excitement of the way it all came together. I had noticed that a few other machines had dropped a load as well. I wondered if Becky had anything to do with that, so I asked her. She told me no, it's just like a ballgame, with all the energy in the place, the excitement of everybody wanting the same thing and waiting until the time is right to strike.

Becky finished her drink, stood up and said, "The night is young. Let's hit the strip and have some fun. Every joint here has live music or slot machines. Maybe we can stir up more excitement someplace else."

I knew the wigwam was Becky's favorite place. That was where she always stayed, and she was friends with all the staff. She must have something special planned that she's not telling anybody about. I have not been disappointed with anything she's suggested, and I have a feeling I'm not going to be. I stood up and said, "Okay, let's do it, I am ready for whatever you can find or have in mind."

We ended up at the Moonlight Bar. this was the early 60s and segregation was a hot topic. But not really being enforced on the strip. For example, there were persons of color at the wigwam every now and then on the entertainment side. Sometimes a member of the kitchen help or maybe the housekeeping department would have one or two. Contrary to the establishment's name there were no Native American Indians. There were, however, several different statues, properly attired and placed conveniently for atmospheric enhancement.

It was kind of like rule of thumb, or mindset, everybody knew where they wanted to be. They also knew where they should or should not go. Except for musicians and music lovers, those lines were very seldom crossed. Though as sad as it may seem, even with those exceptions, a cloud of frictional unrest seemed always to be present.

The Moonlight Bar was predominantly an all Black or person of color establishment. They, to my knowledge, very seldom had White entertainment or band members. The Moonlight Bar had some of the greatest entertainers, especially when it came to the"Blues".

We had a hard time finding a parking place because the parking lot was full. We finally ended up parking under a tree and off the actual parking lot at what seemed like a mile from the front door. On our way to the entrance, we were entertained by several people, all of which were friendly and paid very little attention to us. They were either standing by or leaning up against or sitting on their automobiles. Some had guitars and were singing, others were kinda of dancing, some were drinking. It kinda made the statement that this is where the party's at. As we got to the entrance the door swung open and this big black doorman, which later I found out was the owner, grabbed Becky and gave her a big hug and said," Becky baby, where the hell have you been? Every time this damn door opens I expect you to walk through." Becky laughed, returning a little jiggle to the hug and kiss on the cheek, then said, "Honey, you know what it takes to get me here every night."

I had not been made privy as to what kind of relationship the two of them enjoyed. So I felt it best to watch, let it play out and make my assessment of what was obviously more than a customer to owner acquaintance. I must admit my curiosity had been aroused a little by the type of reception they had for each other, and the next move only aroused it more. He put his arm around Becky's shoulder and said. "Tell your friends to follow us, Babe it's so good to see you.

How long has it been? Maybe I should just lock the doors so I know you'll be here tomorrow when I wake up. Then I won't have to start missing you all over again. Becky responded with, "You come up with some pretty good lines. It just makes me feel all warm and gushy inside. I miss you almost as much as you say you miss me, so fix it. You've got what it takes."

We ended up in what could probably be described as a private penthouse office above the second floor. There were two-way mirrored windows that had been properly placed for overlooking the entire establishment. He had private telephone lines, or intercoms, to the farther away areas and sported a pair of binoculars hanging around his neck. I guess it was so he could entertain his guests, have a few drinks, and at the same time oversee his domain.

The Moonlight bar was a very large place, most likely, because it was the only one of its kind on the strip. I was surprised to see there were no slot machines, especially since Becky wanted to go there. I suppose she had other reasons, maybe she just wanted to give Jennifer and I a grand tour of the strip. There were plenty of card tables along with several crap tables.

After he had taken about five minutes scanning the area with his binoculars, and calling a couple of supervisors, Becky introduced us all. His name was Ron, but Becky referred to him as Ronnie. We had a casual getting to know each other conversation for a few minutes. When, quite suddenly, Becky and Ron slipped into a private room off to the back of his control tower. They were gone for quite some time but I didn't hear any screaming so I felt they must be discussing business dealings. Upon their return Becky said with a smile, "Come on guys, there are no slot machines here, let's go have some fun." Jennifer and I conveyed our nice to meet you Ronnie's, while Becky said her goodbyes with a hug and a kiss-peck to the cheek and I'll see you later baby. We were quietly but expeditiously escorted, by two of Ronnie's understudies, in search of a better word for bouncers. They led us to the front of the establishment facing the parking lot. As we stepped outside and started walking toward the car Becky very quietly said, "Act and walk normal but don't doddle, I'll explain when we get to the car."

As she started the car and pulled away from the parking spot Becky seemed to be little nervous. While she was trying to light a cigarette she said, "That dumb-ass Ronnie! He's such a great guy and I love him, but he has not one fucking idea how to run a business and get along with people. He really scares me. I am afraid he is going to mess around and get himself killed. I hope not, but I do know I don't want to be around if it happens."

As we pulled out onto the main drag going through Waldorf, she gave us somewhat of an explanation. It seemed that while they were in Ronnie's private office, he received a phone call.

And she could tell by the verbiage and tone he used during the call that we should not be at the Moonlight Bar much longer. In other words, she expected there was going to be trouble and that is not the kind of trouble included in mine and Jennifer's training program. I guess that was the first time I realized Jennifer and I were there for the same reasons. Then Becky said, "You guys are going to owe me your lives. Not only for your training program, but for nights like this when I really do save your lives. You do know the only type of payment I expect is a lifetime of lovemaking any time or any place I ask for it." She pulled back into the wigwam parking lot and said, I am as nervous as a whore in church, and I feel worthless as tits on a boar hog. So, in case you're wondering what the hell were doing here, I expect both of you to serve as my doctor and nurse and cure whatever the hell this feeling my body is going through. In other words, we are going back to that big bed. And this time it is my turn to relax and enjoy every possible act of making love you'll can come up with." I said, "Damn Becky, I didn't know you smoked." She replied" I don't, except in times like this, but now you know what you're in for."

Jennifer had a smile on her face that went from ear to ear. She never said a word she just kept smiling all the way to the room. She unlocked and opened the door for Becky. Becky immediately grabbed her by the hand, almost lifting her off the floor in her hot pursuit of horizontal positioning for pleasure and relaxation. I, on the other hand, chose to allow them a little time together to get undressed and warmed up.

I fixed everybody a drink of what I could remember being there favorite. By the time I got the drinks fixed and carried them over to the little table at the head of the bed, Miss unknown, rather Jennifer, and Becky had totally stripped naked. That included necklaces, bracelets, and all rings, even the ones in their ears. I noticed it because they had placed the jewelry pieces of their attire on the little table where I sat our drinks. I thought that was kind of strange but maybe Becky had something new and different in mind for this evening that would help her become more relaxed and take her mind off what was bothering her.

I started to walk over to the couch and sit down and take my shoes off when I heard Becky say. "Just where the hell do you think you're going, you bring that sweet little country ass over here and put it on the bed. Remember I said doctor and nurse, not nurse only. So get ready to play your part Dr. Brent."

While I was taking off my clothes one of them smacked me on the ass with their hand. I thought it was Becky because it felt a little larger and was kind of a forceful gesture to inform me my presence was required.

As I turned around, I noticed they both were visually devouring my cock and nut-sack. It was playing its usual rock-hard and sticking straight out like a piece of wood status. Also, it was beginning to secrete and drool a little. Becky immediately grabbed my cock, sat up and ever so eagerly engulfed it with her mouth. Then she began a soft caressing and rolling the rim process with her tongue to my peckers head. Removing it with a slow sucking loose lip lock while sensually looking up at me with those big almost black eyes and saying, "We can't let that go to waste, it's just too good, and oh so sweet. It must be from all that pussy you eat doctor. You have got a really king-size thermometer doc, and I have a very lonely, empty, and painful feeling in my vaginal canal. Maybe you should take its temperature, in other words, fill that emptiness with your prick and fuck me. Fuck me fast, fuck me deep and fuck me hard. Fuck me to tears Doctor Brent!"

It was as though Becky was putting a personal vendetta approach to this sexual encounter. It must have been so that she could achieve a break-even point with pleasure and pain. She had been a whole different person with a totally different attitude since her rendezvous with her friend at the Moonlight Bar. It was like she was angry but wanted to feel pain at the same time.

As I slipped into position to mount her she grabbed my ass with both hands and pulled me so hard and far inside of her I thought my cock was going to come out of her mouth. Becky winced a little from the ecstasy of it all and at the same time bit Jennifer's tiny little nipple with force enough to make a red mark. As Jennifer screamingly announced her pain Becky began weeping, shaking and coming at the same time. She immediately began hugging both of us and broke into a break-down bawling session.

It appeared as though the lovemaking session was over for the night. Jennifer and I immediately fell into position and began consoling her. We administered a 20 finger tap-walking massage. With soft sensual strokes to all areas of sensitivity, supplying her body with connecting tingles of shock-wave sensations for the sexually oriented areas including her esophagus. My "God", I hadn't noticed before but Becky had one of the biggest esophagus's I had ever had the privilege of looking at from this position. It, all of a sudden, in my mind became a sex organ. As I started to rub my fingers softly up and down over the little ribs on her esophagus, I felt this sudden burning desire to see just how far I could run my cock and balls down her throat. I continued to provide it with a finger-loving masturbation motion. From the position I was in it looked as big around as a stovepipe. It reached in width almost from the left side to the right side of her jaw-bone structure. And in length, from under her chin all the way down to where her cleavage began. There it would lay invisibly tucked away under her breastplate.

While I remained in suspense, still wondering how far down that damn thing goes. I really wanted to know. Becky must have either, read my mind or got excited from the attention I had been giving her esophagus, or knew what I was thinking and wanted it to happen also. She raised her head a little and said, "Prance that pretty-pompous-prick up here and feed me, mama's getting hungry. Let me have a taste of your gargantuan-grandeurs featured flavors."

I began skip-stepping my cock up and down and across her stomach. I popped her bellybutton a couple times then returned to skip-stepping my prick providing more slipperiness from the seepage of my fossil's fuel. I moved up slowly and began nipple bopping, first one and then the other. Then suddenly I grabbed both of her perfectly proportioned medium size tits, pulled them together and dropped my nut sack and cock deep into (**"The Valley Of The Dolls,"**) where I cranked my motor for a mini-motion titty-fuck. It provided such a sexy scene I could not help but give her esophagus and external lube-job.

I repositioned my body and turned around so that I could lay my balls down right on the top of her nose. Becky started moving around a little as though she wanted to get involved. I said, "Ah—ah-ah, you must relax, enjoy, and let the doctor operate."

Jennifer was kind of busy sucking Becky's toes, while playfully massaging her inner thigh and pussy lips. I placed one hand on either side of Becky's middle torso, leaned forward and with a little upper leg muscle lifted my motor slightly. I was positioned for a perfect point of entry with my prick to her esophagus. I could feel her tongue massaging the head of my penis. I thought she might enjoy a little slow-motion lip-pecker waltzing massage in preparation for tunnel travel. I backed out slowly rubbing my balls over her nose as I made my semi-exit and prepared for reentry. I dropped my balls on her lips. Becky's mouth provided an immediate opening for her nut-sack-snack and began sucking on both my balls in a devouring juggling like manner.

She was supplying serious suction. Such an intensely severe sucking force it almost seemed like my balls were being individually vacuumed. I could feel little pains running through my left nut, which to this day is the more sensitive one of the two. I think she may have given me a nut hickey I didn't check to see. All I know is, while she was savagely sucking my balls her nose was preparing for entry in my ass-hole. Eventually I succeeded in backing my balls out of her mouth, again letting them rest on her nose. I immediately felt her hand caress- jerking my cock. I dropped a load that glanced off her chin and hit Jennifer on the cheek. She quickly took her hand, wiped it off and began sucking her fingers.

Once again the thought crossed my mind of what a wonderful place I had discovered. It seemed to be all about love and making love. Trying to remain true to my zodiac love sign and complete the number position,(69), I tried to set my sights on a mouth to pussy process. My prick was perfectly positioned and eagerly awaiting its esophagus adventure. I lowered my ass and pushed my cock-rocket deep into Becky's throat feeling every rib of her esophagus on the way down. Both her hands were on my ass cheeks pulling me farther in. Using one hand she tucked both my balls in her mouth and swallowed my entire shaft. My cocks head must have been resting close to her upper cleavage. I tried to look and see if there was any inner body movement but there was none, so I continued my mouth to pussy lips connection. I started gently kiss-pecking her belly and massaging her bellybutton with my tongue as I tried to line up my path of travel. Since her pussy had been shaved, I could see very clearly where I wanted to go.

Jennifer had progressed from toe sucking to upper inner thigh kiss-biting while her fingers separated Becky's pussy lips to provide a perfect landing for my tongue in her pussy parlor. It was obvious Jennifer was totally in tune with me in creating an evening of relaxation, satisfaction, and enjoyment for our fucking, cock sucking, pussy eating, clit cracking, ah hell, "lovemaking instructor." I glanced down at Jennifer only to find that her position had changed. She was now taking an orgasmic ride on Becky's leg while with one hand spreading her pussy lips and lubricating her middle finger with of the other hand with her own love lava. As my lips made contact with the inner lining of Becky's pussy, Jennifer was proceeding to lubricate Becky's anal area. My cock was taking the trip of its life feeling its way around Becky's tubular throat tunnel. My nuts felt like they were being turned into confetti. I had fired more shots than a crook in a corner with an Uzi, and Becky just kept sucking.

Meanwhile back at the snatch patch, it looked like Jennifer was trying to beat my time with Becky's pussy. She had worked her face up Becky's inner thigh and was hand gesturing me to hold back. As I lifted my head Jennifer buried her face and Becky's pussy and began a vigorous tongue ride on the rim of her entire opening. It was as though she was laying out the tools to make way for me to preform major surgery on Becky's scrumptiously naked, beautifully wide open, tantalizingly invitational lust-filled pussy-hole. After Jennifer had thoroughly announced her pussy presence she began nibble nipping Becky's clit. Then she slid her tongue back and forth on the slippery sloped area that had been formed by the butt crack leading from Becky's ass-hole to her pussy.

Now with both guns aimed and ready for firing I tried to swallow Becky's clitoris. Jennifer buried her middle finger while administering the popping of Becky's prune. I came again, Becky came, I felt it hit me in the nose. I had no idea she could shoot like that, but I'm glad she did. I don't know if Jennifer came but I think she did. Because she was much more energetic with her rodeo maneuvers on Becky's leg and continuing to lick-suck off the free-flowing orgasmic juices from her other hand. Jennifer was eagerly scooping up some of the spare **KUM DROPS** that had splashed from whatever volcano had exploded last.

Once again, I must say this was all beyond my wildest dreams, but apparently not Becky's. She took one hand off my ass-cheek, reached down and got Jennifer by the inner thigh and pulled her around into position where she could reach her pussy. Becky proceeded to lubricate her entire hand and inserted her thumb in Jennifer's pussy and her middle finger in her ass-hole. At which time Jennifer broke into a jump-squirm sort of movement. The more she jumped and squirmed the more her finger moved with a reaming rotation in and out of Becky's anal opening. Becky and Jennifer began moving and shifting, moaning violently while releasing different inner sounds of ecstasy. This of course had to mean that I was moving and shifting violently while they were making those unusual sounds. I was informed later the sounds were referred to as(pussy-farts.) Apparently, they were caused by too much air buildup in the vaginal canal. I had never heard of that before, but the sounds enhanced and demanded more excitement for the act.

Everyone was coming over and over, it was so obvious. Suddenly I felt Jennifer around the side of my face. She had been kissing on Becky's leg, but now had shifted to my earlobe. She was running her tongue all around in the little crevices of my ear as though she were reaming out a pussy. She would ream a little then form her tongue into a point in shove it deep in towards my eardrum. When she would pull out it would make a slap-popping sound. What a hell of a trio, one crazy way to manage the twat's. I am sure glad I'm here instead of home. I was deeply infatuated and oozing with appreciation for the way they were teaching me to play the slots. And the many different ways of approaching the many different slots, as well as the split-open-holes between their legs.

All of a sudden I felt a little harder than a nibble-bite on my ear. At that same time Jennifer seemed to raise about a foot in the air which naturally, when she came down to earth Becky's pussy came up with such force it almost swallowed my face. Fortunately, I was in a position to see part of what I was told later created the dual eruptions. I guess Becky had felt like she needed a little more excitement. So she intentionally sought deeper penetration of her middle finger into Jennifer's ass-hole. This quite naturally raised Jennifer's entire body to an unbelievably satisfying height. Not to mention the almost loss of my ear.

Upon Jennifer's return to her previous position she completely submerged, and I mean out of sight her middle finger in our wonderfully beautiful and oh so caring teachers butt-hole. This of course prompted more violent screams of ecstasy from the two of them. I would have screamed to but I was too busy trying to position each nostril at different times so I would be able to breathe and still continue to perform one of the most breathtaking pussy eating events I have ever had the pleasure of being a part of. Nor did I want to interrupt my trip through the tunnel of esophagus love. The reason it had appeared to be so difficult was when Becky made her landing she almost popped my prune with her nose and drove me almost into smotherasation with a one-way ticket to vagina heaven. I believe it probably goes without saying everybody was very well lubricated and being more lubricated by each other with every passing second. Still, Jennifer would always make sure that nothing went to waste.

I was unaware of it at the time, but apparently Jennifer had experienced somewhat of an unusual pain from her last introduction to rectal rocking. She somehow made Becky aware of that. As a result almost sudden changes of position were taking place under Becky's handling. Handling is the best word to explain it my esophagus excursion came to a very abrupt halt with a smack on my ass from Becky. The only delay of my tubular tunnel trip came as my balls were being slowly assisted while exiting her lips. It seemed like she needed an extra nanosecond with them for a pleasuring cultural suck.

I came to the conclusion there must be a closer connection with Jennifer and Becky than I was aware of. It was kind of like Becky had taken Jennifer under her wing. She was going to make sure that Jennifer was well taken care of and enjoyed everything she was doing. At the time I didn't know, nor did I care. I was there to learn, enjoy, and make sure others enjoyed as well.

In a matter of seconds Jennifer's tight little twat-lay tantalizingly twisted somewhat in front of my mouth. She appeared to be impatiently awaiting for services to be rendered by the titillating treatment of my traveling tongue. It had taken the place of Becky's fantastically juicy, scrumptiously edible pussy. I of course, being a trainee had no other desire than to take care of the task that lay in front of me, and pleasure said pussy with pride.

Eating pussy has always been a pleasure for me. I believe it must have started when I was five years old. One of my older cousins that I had always looked up to and liked to hang around with called me a little cunt-licker. I had no idea what to cunt-licker was, but it did not take me long to find out. Our next-door neighbor had two little girls. One was my age, the other one a couple years older. The older one told me what it was and taught me how to do it. Both of them often played an important part in the transforming of my love for cunt-licking to lust for pussy-eating. And from that day forward eating pussy has always been my favorite dessert. I have loved and took great pride in pleasurably devouring pussy. And still on occasion partake in dreams of afterglow.

I noticed Becky was not only hand gesturing but drawing pictures and making notes. She was proceeding to re-create the "69" position for Jennifer and myself. With a little assistance to her hand signaling, and from notes and images on the notepad, her objective had been achieved and I ended up on the bottom. Becky had been paying particularly special attention to Jennifer since she had experienced a painful poop-shoot. She had stayed kind of busy for a few minutes kissing Jennifer around on different parts of her body and massaging her shoulders, boobies and her pretty little butt-hole. From my newly formed position as the bottom body of a (69'er) I had a perfect view of the entrance to the place of Jennifer's pain. Being a caring and eager to please partner, I offered to assist Becky with her painful prune massage.

While caring for and attending to and trying to lessen the pain of Jennifer's overstretched, almost baby looking butt-hole, Becky had applied some sort of very slippery and soothing lotion or oil to soften and soothe Jennifer's stretched out of shape butt-rim skin. Jennifer was partially supporting her body weight with her knees and upper thighs. Both my hands were free to perform the gentle finger stroking back and forth, around and around on the slippery surface in the valley provided by her butt-cheeks. This was all taking place exactly as Becky had instructed me to do. Jennifer seemed to be enjoying it, so it must be working. She had started swaying her hips left and right which provided more movement and pleasure from her pussy changing position on my lips and tongue she must not have been as secure as Becky with the razor when she was shaving her pussy. I could feel little stubble scratching my nose, which for some strange reason heightened my desire to spread and dive deeper into her tiny-little-twat.

I noticed Becky had been moving around on the bed. I realized later she had picked out a couple sex tools. I suppose she thought they may come in handy later, and she was right. I am still amazed at how she knew just how and what to do at precisely the right time. That's just another reason I'm glad she was my sex trainer.

While I was busying myself deep snatch diving, be-knowing and being the embellisher of Jennifer's cute little butt hole, Becky had made her way to the other end of the "69". There she could cuddle a little, kiss, and console Jennifer to make up for the pain she had caused. Although she cried a little, I do not think Jennifer was too upset. She seemed to be getting right back into the swing of things.

Becky had started kissing Jennifer on the forehead and cheek, then moved down a little closer to my shaft area as it entered Jennifer's mouth. I could feel Becky's famous soft tongue licking exterior shaft massage taking place as Jennifer would slip her lips back while sucking my cock. The next thing I know Becky had caressed my prick with her hand. This induced the immediate draining of my main vein. Jennifer's mouth was still in control of the head of my cock and she began riding the rim with her tongue. I was shooting like a rocket. That resulted in an outpouring of love juices at both corners of Jennifer's mouth. Apparently she could not swallow it fast enough and with no way to transfer it to Becky's face my excrement's were starting to drain down over both sides of Jennifer's chin. Somehow by muffle-mumbling she made Becky aware of it. Becky had absolutely no problem providing quick response and the total recovery of Jennifer's flood zone. Becky transferred most of the excess KUM-juices to my anal area for lubrication. My ass was bouncing around like crazy. Poor little Jennifer was trying to continue her cock-rimming procedure while Becky raised my butt up in the air with her other hand and swallowed my balls. Hence another eruption, it was my turn to scream, and scream I did. Becky consoled me in the only way I wanted. She was squeeze-milking my prick while nibble-nipping and suck-biting my balls and her thumb had found its way to the entrance of my ass-hole.

I was on Mars, or the Moon. I had no idea where I was. All I knew was I was so in to eating that pussy and coming, that I did not realize I had a little too much pressure on my finger as it followed Jennifer's butt-crack and dropped it right into her anal-opening. She bit into my main vein and I screamed and jerked a little as my mouth and tongue began feverishly massaging her pussy. Jennifer reciprocated by kiss sucking the head of my cock and main vein. Becky involved herself more by milking faster, sucking harder and holding it longer. I wasn't paying any attention to anybody else. All I knew was that I was doing the shotgun boogie, shooting over and over. I figured I had choked Jennifer by this time, but she was still riding the rim with her tongue and kiss pecking the head of my cock. I eased my finger out of her ass-hole and gently started a reaming massage motion on her perfect little prune. Then, smothering her clitoris with my tongue I continued my due diligence by slurping her into a semi-bounce rock 'n roll motion with her buttocks on my face. Jennifer's body greeted her with an orgasmic-burst that could have been a double-first-cousin to a volcano. It was a true sign of total appreciation for a job being done well.

Becky pushed her hand farther up my shaft to Jennifer's lips, forcing her to relinquish possession of the head of my cock. Becky kept one hand on my prick while pushing my butt a little farther up in the air with the other one, bringing Jennifer's mouth closer to my nut-sack. I heard her whisper to Jennifer, "Come on up here honey and help me out with this. Brent has been a pretty good sport, let's tear his ass up. We will double his pleasure and double his fun but try to keep his pain on the good side. Remember, we rehearsed this one a couple times." Suddenly my ass felt like it was on an elevator and had just moved one floor up. That maneuver, of course, brought Jennifer's pussy crashing down on my face with twice the force. At the precise time of the crash she performed a perfect saddle-split, which almost enabled me to succeed in going somewhere I have always wanted to go.

I remember many times thinking how once upon a time I had been formed inside and came out of this unbelievably wonderful sexy body part, and some-day I would return to the place of my birth. The driving desire to deliver that dream was so overwhelming. All I could think of was, that pussy, that twat, that snatch, that cunt, was the open door for a pathway to paradise in a vagina valley to finally be my resting place. The thought of taking that dive and making a successful entrance totally consumed my being.

I was unfortunately brought back to my senses by the sudden seepage of sexually aroused secretions filling my nostrils while trying to bury myself in the lotions of love. What a damn disappointment, still I continued on course, hoping for some sort of intercoursal intervention that might permit at least partial submergence. I have never felt more comfortable and at the same time more out of control, than when I was close to or partaking of pussy, especially the submissive ones. I thought Becky had the best pussy in the world. Especially with her little added attractions she would subject you to. But it seemed like Jennifer had consumed an overdose of candy, ice cream, cake, and pie, all filled with sugar and released the sweetest most abundant overflow of orgasmic juices through a four-course meal of sweet sexual secretions. So much so that I thought I might be overcome by a pussy-coma. I realized at that time, there was no best pussy. All pussy is good, it is all about how good you are at getting them to perform with you.

I had not been able to see for about 20 minutes. That was when the elevation process began and I lost sight of Jennifer's anal orifice. Nor had I been able to comfortably breathe without snorkeling pussy juices for the past 10 minutes or so. Now, I realize my head is so far up between her thighs the overflowing fluids are streaming down her inner thighs and off my cheeks into my ears. That would be three of my six senses. I don't care what they do to my prick, my balls, my ass-hole, or any sexual maneuver that could possibly be accomplished. I love the taste of love. But I long to see the performance and hear the slushing sounds of sex as it surrounds my sense of smell while smothering all other senses and you are left in limbo. Somewhat brain-dead for the duration of whatever act of love is being preformed.

All of a sudden everything was interrupted by the ringing of a phone. That was a different sound. I did not realize the room had a phone. I guess Becky didn't want to answer it. She waited for it to stop ringing then reached over and pulled the drawer of the night stand out. She took the receiver off the hook and laid it down beside the phone and shut the drawer. Acting as though nothing happened, she returned to her persuasive ways of continuing mine and Jennifer's training program.

I heard kind of like a buzzing noise and felt a vibrating tickle sensation around my ass-hole, balls and the main vein area of my shaft. It provided me with the longest lasting orgasmic explosion of love lotion I think I had ever experienced. That was followed by a savagely-sucking, lip-lock to the head of my cock by Jennifer's hungry and seemingly **KUM-starved** mouth. Which caused another continuous coming stream of secretions. I wondered where it was all coming from. It felt like she was sucking my brains out. If what some people say is true, all your brains are in the head of your cock, I am sure she would have sucked them all out by now.

The excitement from it all was releasing an occasional exotically-erotic, ecstasy-filled pain throughout my entire body, especially my scrotum area. Everything was being laid out on a big-bed stage. Performed on some unknown sex starved planet of pussy's and directed by the sweetest most lovably thoughtful erotomaniac ever born. There I was, wondering around in outer space again.

Suddenly my whole body stiffened into a potential an uncontrollable cramping mode, resulting in me not being able to straighten my toes. I was probably getting dehydrated. Becky must've taken notice to what was happening with my body's shaking sensation and toe-locking. She quietly and undisturbedly turned over the Swedish massage machine with its feathery-fan to Jennifer. Who was not only very competent but anxiously awaiting the opportunity to exhibit her expertise in this particular part of her training.

Becky had reversed her position to the point she was almost an extension of Jennifer's body. Her ass cheeks and anal-opening was almost touching Jennifer's forehead. Her oversized but firm tummy was caressing my knees. I believe she purposely planned it so that her ever so tantalizing tits would rest on the lower shin and upper ankle area of my legs. This allowed her to pay attention to my cramping areas. While resting most her upper body weight on her elbows she began the gentle massaging procedure on my toes and the instep areas of my feet. The true tools of Becky's trade were her hands, fingers, and tongue, and of course, those always inviting seductive lips. It turned out to be the craziest fantastically fucking dream position one could ever hope for.

Becky was extraordinarily attentive when it came to Jennifer, or me. She always made sure there was a part of her body to place on or partake of a part of our bodies. Hell, with the head of my cock in Jennifer's mouth while she was performing a beautiful massage with a motorized feather-duster on my nut-sack and anal-area I was trying to titty-fuck Becky with my shin bone. At the same time she was paying special attention to my feet and toes while surrendering slip-sucking slurping sounds of sex.

We had gradually adjusted our positions to more of a diagonal like from top corner too far bottom corner of the beds. This had become necessary while we were becoming a three-in-one, or maybe I should say as the three of us became one. Over the next few orgasmic-like earth shattering minutes Jennifer continued to perform miracles with the feather-fan and vibrated my rocks off several times. During that time she was administering a double-dose of Becky's preferred pleasures within her rectal reach.

If I stop to think about it now, I can only dream about how it used to be. I can settle for that. Although I'm not crazy enough to think I could still perform at that same level. But I am crazy enough to die trying.

When I awoke Jennifer had gone to the other room to take a shower. Becky had a mouthful of what she had proclaimed her favorite mushroom. Softly and tenderly she brought me back to life and assured her favorite inserted dominant topside ride. Then she informed me from a rock-a-bye baby still love ya maybe position, "You should probably take a shower maybe try to freshen up a little because we are going to get company. But not before I'm ready to let you go. You are beginning to become a habit." Becky loved all positions of sex but especially that one. It was her position of dominance and control.

After a few minutes of sleepy slippery sex, accompanied by what information she thought I might need about our new arrival. She leaned forward, slipped off and when the air hit the head of my cock it was like a soft painful cooling sensation provided by the surrendering control of her hot box. Becky placed her hand around my shaft to secure the warmth, leaned up and presented me with a loving kiss of appreciation. Then as she was leaving the bed bent over and sensually suck-molested my cock's head and said,

"Emm-mmm, I love this thing, and if you don't quit fucking around I'm going to fall in love with you." She slapped me hard on the hip and said as she left the bed. "Go get a shower and wake up. You've got a few minutes before your next lesson starts."

I may have been tired but I didn't feel that way. While I was taking a shower, I couldn't help wondering or thinking who was going to be arriving next? What were the sexual possibilities? It succeeded in waking me, while filling my mind with all kinds of interesting tid-bits of damn I wish I knew. That was just another way of Becky's playing her part as the trainer. She felt surprise was always the most important commodity and would almost always bust a nut.

When I got out of the shower and was drying off, I could hear voices, but the only one I recognized was Becky's. Thinking there would be very little need for me to get dressed I grabbed a large towel and secured it around my waist. I opened the door and stepped out into the room only to find three fully clad young ladies. I started walking towards a closet with the intention of finding some clothes when I heard three voices in unison saying, "No, you won't need those." I glanced towards Becky and she was laughing. So I figured what the hell, this is what I'm here for and walked over and sat down on the edge of the bed. It was Becky, Jennifer, and Becky's friend Sandy.

Sandy had apparently been the one who called. Becky must have returned her call after I passed out. We all got reacquainted and I once again was appointed bartender. I took their orders and proceeded to fix drinks. We all took a few minutes to gather ourselves and create a more relaxed atmosphere. From the conversation that followed it appeared that Sandy had experienced some difficulty since the last time we met. I was not however, privy to what that might have been. As it turns out it didn't matter much anyway. We finished our drinks and cordially complemented each other. One thing I did find out was that Sandy was not in a training program.

The bed had been freshly made and assembled in the same manner as before, an additional night stand had been placed at the foot of the bed.

Everybody was in need of another drink, so I attended to my responsibilities.

Sandy and Jennifer, with nodded approval to follow Becky's lead, began removing their clothes in a rather invitational manner. Blouses, skirts and slacks, panties and bras, of course, Jennifer wasn't wearing a bra. This made her time travel to nudity much faster. Becky while undressing had returned to her habit of towel-tugging. This of course, rendered me naked with a hard-on. Becky gently slid her hand around my shaft and gave my balls a very cordial rolling squeeze. The first thing I thought of was, now that is a hairy pussy. It made it very obvious to me that Sandy had not been involved in the pussy shaving process. She had a fur-burger that left everything for the imagination. It was so heavy and thick you couldn't even see the parting place for her pussy lips. It was just a big spectacular triangular piece of hair. Compared to the others it almost looked like a pussy wig. For some strange reason it had become somewhat of a turn-on to me.

I believe Becky realized that because she saw me concentrating on Sandy's fur-peace. She knew I wanted to go there first regardless of the outcome of my next trip to the dentist. Becky winked at Sandy and it was a done deal. What a fantastic assignment was before me. Properly fitting the pieces to this pussy puzzle was a job I was really looking forward to.

There was Becky with her queen-size body. She had jet black hair and absolutely beautiful facial features and possessed the softest, most lust-filled, cock and ball massaging mouth and tongue. Complemented to the highest by an esophagus that made this statement, "I will turn your prick into a repeating rifle if you travel this tunnel of love." Becky had a set of tits that demanded attention with their succulent nipples and South American, maybe Asian style, dark overlay area. Her nipples were damn near as big as Jennifer's tittys. Then comes her hourglass shaped lower rib cage and tummy which sets up a perfect view of her firing line. Especially after being involved in the pussy shaving process. From there leading into the bottom part of the hourglass was her lower torso. The curves of her upper and inner thighs trailing to her calf's flowing gracefully to the tips of her out-stretched toes, made all other torso travel time seems slow. As long as I knew Becky, I never got tired of the time it took for me to totally view and appreciate every fraction of an inch of her beautiful body.

Next, we have Jennifer with her semi-male mohawk haircut and very attractive face. Her pretty little mouth with lips she was learning to use quite well. Her body was straight and resembled a fencepost with two of the cutest little pine-knot-nipples. I liked and enjoyed playing with her, easy to manage and very succulent, little tiny tittys. I could zero in on them without thinking they were going to get away. Her entire body was just a very petite fuck. Or maybe I should categorize her as being a very petite future lovemaking machine. And I loved that pretty little pussy, it was as edible as she was agile.

Fitting perfectly in place for the final piece of this pussy puzzle was Sandy. I had thought about Sandy quite a few times since we first met but really didn't know much about her. I was beginning to find out. She had long kind of wavy blonde hair. Reminded me a little bit of Andrea's. Made me immediately want to jump her bones and tie my cock and balls up with her hair. Then let her try to find and suck it without getting hair in her mouth. Sandy was very well proportioned. She had a very pretty face and nice medium-sized tits. She was a little loose in the tummy with nice hips and legs and a hell of a fur-burger. Overall, Sandy was put together very well. But I was getting anxious since starting to drool with the thought of getting some of those curly little pubic hairs stuck between my teeth and tickling my throat while curling around my tonsils. Hell, I bet if she raised her legs up while I was eating her pussy, I could tickle my ears.

I was trying to put the picture of them together in my mind as one fine superb specimen of female flesh. It was totally irresistible. I was drooling all over my leg. Becky saw what was happening to me and laughingly said, "Quit dreaming Brent, get over here and take care of business." Becky had everybody in place. It made it easy for me to see where I was going. This was one time I could relate to a Ricky Nelson's song, "I'm a Traveling Man." I just wondered if he did it this way.

The Pickering order was similar but not quite the same as a previous lesson. Becky was kind of semi-sit-laying with her back to the wall. Sandy and Jennifer were on either side of her. Totally devouring her armpits nipples and tummy. My destiny had been predetermined I would be furr-diving for the pearl.

It must have appeared as though I did not want to waste any time. With very little foreplay except for the lip finding process and providing a pubic hair split, I went straight for my favorite pussy eating position (69'er). I immediately buried my face and began a pussy lip massage with a tantalizing tongue tipping to her clit. Sandy was ripe and ready. She was moving and squirming from side to side. It was easy to tell that I was in for a good ride.

Becky had her friendly little cat-of-nine-tails whip trailing in ticklish fashion across my butt with an occasional slap. I felt a hand on my left butt-cheek. It must have been Jennifer. Suddenly I felt Sandy's hand on my right butt-cheek. Then with the whip-tickling and slapping process I felt my butt-crack and anal-opening being lubricated with both Jennifer and Sandy's hands. Influenced by these proceedings I lubricated every digit on my right hand with love-lotion excrement's, from Sandy's pussy. Sandy immediately responded by raising her butt just a little and I stuck my left hand under it to maintain that position. I then started my ass-crack and butt-hole tongue-soothing massage on Sandy's silky but slippery rear entrance. She began to move in a shaky squirm like manner. Letting me know she very much approved of rear entry.

I had been tongue-lapping her extremely fuzzy pussy, the juices were flowing. I felt a rather violent slap of the whip on my ass along with Jennifer's finger reaming my ass-hole. Another slap and my finger slipped into Sandy's previously lubricated prune, she immediately started almost jump-shaking. We were all moving with the same rhythm. Suddenly I felt Jennifer behind me spreading my ass-cheeks. She had the strap-on dill-doe and was ready to rumble. Becky had her whip going back and forth across my ass like a drum solo. I had buried my face deep in Sandy's pussy and was devouring her clitoris. She gave one semi-butt-bounce just as Jennifer entered my ass-hole with her make-believe prick. I gruntingly jerked, popped a nut and Jennifer's hand found it. She immediately transferred the leftovers to Becky's face and mouth while keeping her other hand on my cock. Sandy started quivering and shake-shooting time after time. Becky was whip-slapping everybody and Jennifer was rotating in and out, deeper and deeper into my anal cavity. I don't know how many times I got my rocks. I do know not nearly as many as Sandy did. Sandy acted like she had been on a pussy strike and was starved for climaxes. As fast as they were coming to her, she must have built-up love juices in her Kum-container. I could feel her pussy hairs clogging my nose and tickling my ears as they tangled around my tonsils while traveling to my throat. Her legs were sticking straight up in the air and I was now licking juices from the naturally hairy fuzz-patch-filter provided around her pussy and inner thighs.

I cannot be sure about anybody else, but I know by this time I had already busted my nuts at least five times. Sandy probably 10 or 15 and Jennifer I know had one or two. Becky must've had at least three or four orgasmic surprises. Sometimes it was uncomfortable, but it was offset by the pleasures and the satisfaction of watching everyone enjoy the process.

I wasn't sure exactly what my next move should be. There were a couple things I had come to realize.

I needed to somehow persuade Jennifer and her dill do friend to get the hell out of my ass-hole. I really was not used to that and it was beginning to cause more discomfort than I wanted.

I had noticed that Sandy had been especially excitable when attention was being paid to her butt-crack area and anal-opening. I pushed myself forward slightly brought both my arms in between Sandy's up-stretched legs, took both hands and pulled her into position where my mouth could service both her pussy and her prune. With help from my arms pushing against the inside of her legs I dropped my chin and began to give her a tender tongue treatment in the connecting crevice between her pussy and ass-hole. Sandy responded with a squirting-shake as I slipped my finger out of her butt-hole. I lifted her butt a little higher and replaced a finger with my tongue. She went slap-happy and started shooting all over my chin. I felt her fingernails digging deep into my back while she was pulling my mouth tighter to her lesbian-love-hole. Oops, I slipped, I found out later that Sandy definitely preferred women and the tongue to ass-hole process was her favorite method of molestation.

With a few gradual shifting-rolls of our bodies she became topside. This automatically removed Jennifer's artificial prick from my prune. Sandy could not stop shaking. She pressed her butt tighter and tighter against my face. I spread her ass cheeks as wide open as I could and began a bung-hole-bonding with my lips. Sandy was having little mini-orgasms with every shake. Her upper torso was partly twisted to one side. Still shaking and shooting she started in with a suck-slurping process of eating Becky's pussy. Becky immediately grabbed my cock and started jerking me off. I was shooting straight up in the air, providing Becky with plenty of **KUM** to rub through her hair, on her face and around the nipple area of her tittys. Which, by this time was being orally gratified by Jennifer. She had abandoned the strap-on dill-doe and was partially stan-bending her knees, placing her pussy for the easy access licking of Becky's tongue Jennifer was assisting Sandy by massaging Becky's pussy with one hand and playing with Sandy's tits with the other.

Before I realized what was happening, Jennifer had changed positions and began a somewhat tantalizing but titillating tour of nibbling my nuts. I knew Becky had been working on this maneuver with her, but it was totally unexpected. It felt so good I must have been paying more attention to my nut sucker than the service I was performing for Sandy. She, on no uncertain terms, let me know I was guilty of dereliction of duty. I couldn't help it and I said, "Sandy, baby I'm sorry, but this feels so good I have got to just lay back and enjoy." And that is exactly what I did.

I got the feeling that was okay with everybody because Becky and Sandy fell into a togetherness of their own. The love and affection they displayed for each other in a way provided a turn-on-ish atmosphere for our viewing pleasure. They had come together in what I guess you might call a female (69'er) that kind of resembled a ball. The bed was only large enough for them to roll a short distance. If they had been on the floor, they could have rolled all around the room staying connected. Sandy had the smaller handheld dill-doe adding to the excitement for Becky's ass-hole. Becky was utilizing all the talents of her tongue and fingers in appreciation for Sandy's love for anal molestation.

In the meantime, Jennifer had grabbed a pillow and tucked it up under my ass. She started somewhat of a sloppy spit-sucking one ball at a time process. This allowed her saliva to drain down the crack of my ass and she was following the flow with her tongue for a prune-licking procedure. Jennifer was paying more attention to my nuts and shaft. She would occasionally administer a traveling tongue-lap of my main vein and the head of my cock for a slobbering-suck, then back to my nut-sack. Over the next few minutes Jennifer exhibited an excellent performance of cock-sucking, ball-blazing, and ass-licking, with an occasional double-ball tongue-twirl.

I had already quit counting climaxes. I do know there could have not been much juice left in me. My only hope was that I had been as good a student as Jennifer.

I was suddenly overcome with the desire to hail Jennifer's performance. I leaned forward and grabbed her face with both hands and applied a lip-lock with enough suction to extract her tongue. I gently laid her back until I was on top of her. My eager to please pecker had no problem finding her pussy. We made normal missionary style love for a minute or two. Then I nibble-nipped her left tit as I was easing her up on her right side. I lifted her left leg over my right shoulder and started piledriving her pussy with full motor force. Jennifer began to moan scream, and grunt. I slapped the side of her ass and pumped harder while saying to her, "Thank you baby, now favor me with your most abundant outpouring and pleasurable orgasmic explosion of love's lotion for this final fuck." I pumped harder and harder, deeper and deeper, and with one final plunge of my prick slamming hard against the inner wall lining of her pussy, she screamed as though she was dying, and so did I. We collapsed with a continuous kiss in each other's arms.

Becky and Sandy were silently watching. They both rolled over to us in kind of a congratulatory consoling kiss massaging manner. You could tell from the look in Becky's eyes she was very pleased with our progress.

Becky and Sandy were crying and coming together funny, my thoughts went immediately to Andrea. It must have been because she was the one who taught me to side-saddle-fuck. As I drifted off into a dreamy paradise of afterglow, I was wondering where she was.

Good Night!!!
I hope you have enjoyed the bedtime stories.
It's been fun, we must do this again.

Until then, Pat Parsons

Lightning Source UK Ltd.
Milton Keynes UK
UKHW011840190521
384027UK00001B/40